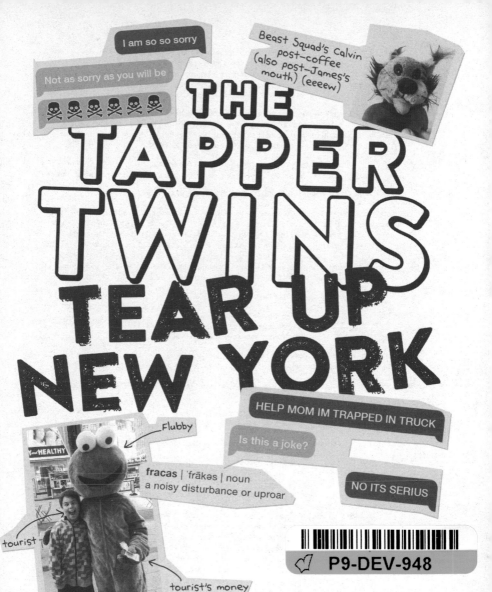

I am so so sorry

Not as sorry as you will be

☠☠☠☠☠☠☠

Beast Squad's Calvin post—coffee (also post—James's mouth) (eeeew)

THE TAPPER TWINS TEAR UP NEW YORK

HELP MOM IM TRAPPED IN TRUCK

Is this a joke?

→ Flubby

fracas | ˈfrākəs | noun
a noisy disturbance or uproar

NO ITS SERIUS

YourHEALTHY

← tourist

tourist's money

P9-DEV-948

GEOFF RODKEY

TOTALLY INSANE

LB
Little, Brown and Company
New York · Boston

Copyright © 2015 by Geoff Rodkey
Excerpt from *The Tapper Twins Run for President* copyright © 2015 by Geoff Rodkey

Page 263 constitutes an extension of this copyright page.

Little, Brown and Company

Hachette Book Group
1290 Avenue of the Americas, New York, NY 10104
Visit us at lb-kids.com

Little, Brown and Company is a division of Hachette Book Group, Inc.
The Little, Brown name and logo are trademarks of Hachette Book Group, Inc.

The publisher is not responsible for websites (or their content) that are not owned by the publisher.

First Paperback Edition: May 2016
First published in hardcover in September 2015 by Little, Brown and Company

The Library of Congress has cataloged the hardcover edition as follows:

Rodkey, Geoff, 1970– author.
The Tapper twins tear up New York / Geoff Rodkey. — First edition.
pages cm. — (Tapper twins ; 2)
Summary: An oral history that reports, through transcribed recordings, text messages, photographs, illustrations, screenshots, and more, on the First (and last) Annual Culvert Prep Middle School Scavenger Hunt For Charity, and the adventures of twelve-year-old twins Reese and Claudia Tapper as their highly competitive teams scour New York for treasure.
ISBN 978-0-316-29783-7 (hardcover) — ISBN 978-0-316-38029-4 (ebook) — ISBN 978-0-316-38028-7 (library edition ebook)
1. Treasure hunt (Game)—Juvenile fiction.
2. Twins—Juvenile fiction. 3. Brothers and sisters—Juvenile fiction.
4. Middle schools—Juvenile fiction. 5. Competition (Psychology)—Juvenile fiction. 6. New York (N.Y.)—Juvenile fiction.
[1. Treasure hunt (Game)—Fiction. 2. Twins—Fiction.
3. Brothers and sisters—Fiction. 4. Middle schools—Fiction.
5. Schools—Fiction. 6. Competition (Psychology)—Fiction.
7. Humorous stories. 8. New York (N.Y.)—Fiction.] I. Title.
PZ7.R61585Td 2015 813.6—dc23 [Fic] 2014040292

Paperback ISBN 978-0-316-31601-9

10 9 8 7 6 5 4
LSC-C

Printed in the United States of America

AN ORAL HISTORY OF THE FIRST ANNUAL CULVERT PREP MIDDLE SCHOOL SCAVENGER HUNT FOR CHARITY

which took place in
New York City, NY
on
Saturday, October 25
(and absolutely DID NOT cause a riot)

interviews conducted by
CLAUDIA TAPPER
with
Reese Tapper
Akash Gupta
Parvati Gupta
Carmen Gutierrez
Sophie Koh
Kalisha Hendricks
Jens Kuypers
Xander Billington
Wyatt Templeman
James Mantolini
Dimitri Sharansky
Toby Zimmerman
Vice Principal Joanna Bevan
Eric S. Tapper, Esquire
And anyone else I forgot

Media inquiries: contact Claudia Tapper
(claudaroo@gmail.com)

Lawsuits/subpoenas/etc: Eric Tapper
(eric.steven.tapper@gmail.com)

CONTENTS

PROLOGUE

CLAUDIA

This is the official history of the First Annual Culvert Prep Middle School Scavenger Hunt For Charity.

I am writing it because there is a WHOLE lot of bad information out there about what happened. Mostly because of that stupid article in the *New York Star*.

NOT TRUE

SCHOOLKID SCAVENGERS RUN RIOT
Private School Kids, Parents In Fundraiser Fracas

(kind of true)

Which was almost completely not true. At NO point did ANYBODY involved in the hunt "run riot."

Except possibly for a couple of minutes at the end. But I can explain that.

And I'll admit that what happened was technically a "fracas." But since almost nobody has any idea what that word means, it's kind of ridiculous to put it in a headline.

Also, some of the things that happened with my brother Reese's team were definitely not good. Or legal.

But overall, the scavenger hunt was a HUGE SUCCESS. We raised $8,748.75 for the Manhattan Food Bank, which is TOTALLY AMAZING. A LOT of hungry people got to eat decent meals thanks to our scavenger hunt.

Not that you'd know any of this from reading the stupid *New York Star*.

Which, again, is why I'm writing this history, based on interviews with everyone involved. Because, as the person who not only had the idea for the hunt but also organized it, all this misinformation has been very painful and frustrating.

except people who wouldn't talk to me

The fact that there will not be a Second Annual Scavenger Hunt—because Vice Principal Bevan has banned them forever—is also very frustrating.

And honestly, I think Mrs. Bevan overreacted. Nobody actually filed a lawsuit. Those were just empty threats.

(so far)

REESE

All I can say is, none of the bad stuff that happened on our team was my fault. Most of the laws we broke, I didn't even know were laws. So those shouldn't count.

And none of it would've happened in the first place if Dad had done a better job of being our team chaperone.

I don't want to throw Dad under the bus or anything. But that was pretty much the whole problem right there.

Mom's still really mad at him for it.

MOM AND DAD (Text messages copied from Mom's phone)

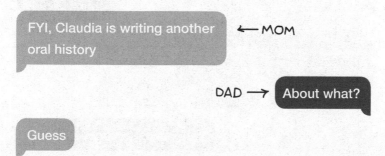

FYI, Claudia is writing another oral history ← MOM

DAD → About what?

Guess

Please tell me it's not scavenger hunt

Bingo

OMG. You're not letting her use our texts again, are you?

why not?

BECAUSE I WILL LOOK LIKE WORST PARENT IN HISTORY

Also worst husband. Don't forget that

I know! I am sorry for 100th time! Please please please don't let C use texts

I won't

thank you!!!!

unless I'm lying. Because we know ALL ABOUT lying to people in text messages, DON'T WE ERIC??

I am so so so very very sorry

I know you are. And I forgive you

so you won't let her use texts, right?

right?

honey?

no comment

Thanks, Mom!

CHAPTER 1
I HAVE AN EXCELLENT IDEA
(WITH A LITTLE HELP
FROM MY BROTHER)

CLAUDIA

    I came up with the idea for the scavenger hunt while taking the M79 bus across Central Park to school.

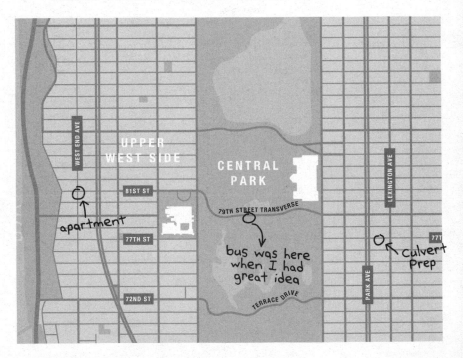

REESE

You didn't come up with it! It was MY idea!

You just ripped it off. And you never once gave me credit!

CLAUDIA

Do you seriously want credit for it? After everything that happened?

REESE

Oh, yeah...Good point. Never mind.

CLAUDIA

By the way, for anyone who doesn't already know, Reese and I are twins.

Which is weird. Because we are not twin-like at all. In fact, we are VERY different.

I don't want to get into HOW we're different, because I believe every person is special and unique—and if you put a label on someone, it's like forcing them into a tiny box where they have no room to move and can't just be themselves.

Which, obviously, is not cool.

Although if I absolutely HAD to put
labels on us, I would be The Smart One.
And Reese would be The Sporty One.
Or possibly The Smelly One.
Or maybe even The One Who Wastes His
Life Playing Video Games While His Sister Is
Busy Trying To Make The World A Better Place.

if we were pets, I would be:

and Reese would be:

See what I mean about labels? They are
very unfair.
Even when they're true.
Back to the M79 bus.

M79 bus = crazy slow
(but faster than walking)
(but not by much)

Reese and I were sitting together, and I was writing a speech for Student Government about my proposal to do a fundraiser for the Manhattan Food Bank.

The fact that some people in New York City don't have enough food to eat REALLY bothers me. Especially when you consider how well off a lot of families at Culvert Prep are. It just seems completely unfair and wrong that kids could go hungry in one part of the city while people like Athena Cohen have so much money they can fly to Bermuda every weekend on a private jet.

And as president, I'd decided I should do something about this.

REESE

You realize you're only president of the sixth grade, right?

Like, you're not president of the whole city?

CLAUDIA

Okay, A) Duh.

B) New York City has a MAYOR, not a president.

NYC mayor lives here
(almost as nice as White House)
(but hard to get good pic due to trees/fence)

And C) have you ever heard the term "Think globally, act locally"?

REESE

Maybe. Was that in a Burger King commercial?

CLAUDIA

I am almost completely sure it wasn't.

REESE

Oh. Then no.

CLAUDIA

That is just sad, Reese. Seriously.
Back to the bus. I was working on my speech. And Reese was babbling about some MetaWorld thing.

REESE

MetaWorld is, like, the greatest video game in the history of the universe. It's not even one game. It's more like fifty different games all skrudged together.

not an actual word

And one of them is MetaHunt, which is this super-massive scavenger hunt. Only it's MUCH cooler than a regular scavenger hunt, because you can kill other players and take all their stuff. So if you kill enough people, you don't even have to find any of the stuff yourself.

MetaHunt looks like this:

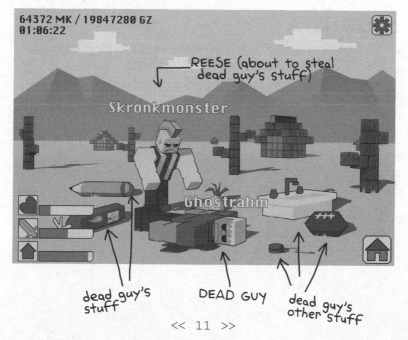

I'd been playing a ton of MetaHunt, and it got me thinking how awesome it'd be to do a scavenger hunt for real all over New York City.

We couldn't, like, actually kill each other. But it'd still be cool.

So when Claudia was like, "Shut up, Reese! I'm writing my Student Government speech!"

I was like, "You should have the SG do a scavenger hunt! For the whole school!"

And Claudia was like, "That is the DUMBEST idea—heeeeey, wait a minute..."

CLAUDIA

And that's basically how it all started.

CHAPTER 4
SCAVENGER HUNT FEVER
GRIPS CULVERT PREP

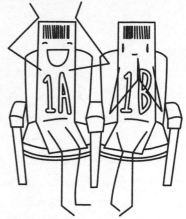

CLAUDIA

So, this is Chapter 4.

You might be wondering why there's no Chapter 2 or 3.

There used to be. And personally, I thought they were fascinating.

But everybody who read the first draft said they were incredibly boring.

Sophie
Parvati
Carmen
Mom

So I got rid of them. But in case you're wondering, Chapter 2 was about the speech I gave that got the Student Government to pass a resolution creating the First Annual Culvert Prep Middle School Scavenger Hunt For Charity.

Not to brag, but it was a very effective speech. I quoted both Miranda Fleet AND Gandhi.

Miranda Fleet: world's greatest singer/songwriter

Gandhi: world's greatest peaceful protester

Chapter 3 was about all the planning we did to put the hunt together. By "we," I mostly mean me and Akash Gupta, my co-chair on the Scavenger Hunt Committee. And also Vice Principal Bevan, because she had to approve everything.

Akash is in eighth grade. He's the (Parvati) older brother of one of my best friends, and he's basically a genius—although tbh, that can make him kind of hard to work with.

AKASH GUPTA, co-chair of Scavenger Hunt Committee

I can't believe you cut Chapter 3! That was the best chapter!

CLAUDIA

I know, right?! But everybody else thought it was death.

AKASH

People are idiots. It's the same way with coding. Everybody wants to play Exploding Cows. But nobody cares how it gets made.

Exploding Cows: totally stupid
(but highly addictive) app

SCORE: 2500

And planning that scavenger hunt was
seriously complicated! Especially after you
quit and I had to do everything myself.

CLAUDIA

I did NOT quit! It's just that once I
decided I wanted to PLAY as well as PLAN the
hunt, Mrs. Bevan made me resign as co-chair
to avoid any appearance of corruption.

AKASH

Oh, sure. Just keep telling yourself that.
Whatever lets you sleep at night, quitter.

CLAUDIA

FYI, this is what I mean when I say Akash can be hard to work with.

Here's what happened: at first, I was not planning to be in the hunt at all. But one of the things Akash and I had to do was come up with prizes for the winning teams.

And since Mrs. Bevan wouldn't let us spend any serious money, second and third prize wound up being kind of lame.

AKASH

I'm sorry, but a $20 Starbucks gift card? When there's four players on a team? It's ridiculous! You can't even get everybody grande Frappuccinos for that kind of money.

And third place was even worse. Those Culvert Prep pencil cases are total crap. They're, like, ten for a dollar.

~~Mrs. Bevan's a complete cheapskate.~~
~~Wait, don't print that.~~

forgot to take this out—sorry, Akash!

CLAUDIA

~~I won't.~~

But first prize was a whole other story. Allegra Bell has a dad with some kind of

big job at Madison Square Garden. And Akash
convinced Allegra to get her dad to donate
four front-row seats to ANY EVENT at the
Garden as a first prize.

MADISON SQUARE GARDEN
(aka the Garden) (aka MSG)

(also, weird
thing:
it's ROUND)

just two
blocks from
Empire State
Building!

Which was completely, insanely,
amazingly, incredibly, and in all other ways
TOTALLY AWESOME.

Because the list of upcoming events at
MSG included not just Knicks games, Rangers
games, and some wrestling thing that a
bunch of the fifth grade boys were into, but
also Fiddy K, Deondra, AND Miranda Fleet
concerts.

Which was huge for me. Miranda Fleet
is not only the world's greatest singer-
songwriter, she's also my idol and the one

person besides the president whose job I
want when I grow up. So the chance to see
her live, from the FRONT ROW...was something
I absolutely did not want to pass up.

Pretty much everybody at Culvert
Prep felt the same way. Once word got out
about the front-row seats, interest in the
scavenger hunt basically exploded.

SOPHIE KOH, best friend of Claudia

People went NUTS for those tickets. It
was all anybody talked about for days.

**PARVATI GUPTA, second-best friend of
Claudia** (tied with Carmen)

Can I just say, when I heard I
could get front-row seats to Deondra? I
practically peed my pants. She is TOTALLY
AMAZING.

**CARMEN GUTIERREZ, second-best friend of
Claudia** (tied with Parvati)

I had a real moral dilemma. Because
I seriously didn't know whether I wanted
to see Miranda Fleet or Deondra more. But
either way, I was all, "SQUEEEEE!"

REESE

At first, a lot of my friends were like, "It's a scavenger hunt—only we can't kill people and take their stuff? What's the point?"

But when they found out they could get free tickets to the Knicks, or Fiddy K, they were like, "BA-DA-ZING!"

↖ not actually a word

WYATT TEMPLEMAN, friend of Reese (also minor idiot)

I was totally psyched. I heard if you sit in the front row at a Knicks game, the players will, like, actually sweat on you. That would be SO sweet. NO IT WOULDN'T (eeeew)

XANDER BILLINGTON, friend of Reese (also MAJOR idiot)

I's all, "FIDDY K IN DA HIZZZZ-OUSE! I'M'A HAMMER DOWN ON DAT!"

Dem free tix wuz BEAST, yo.

CLAUDIA

FYI, it's important to know this about Xander Billington: he's not only a major idiot, he's also from one of the oldest families in America. Apparently, the Billingtons came over from England with the original Pilgrims on the

Mayflower. Whenever I think about this, I feel really bad for the other Pilgrims.

THE LANDING OF THE PILGRIMS AT PLYMOUTH, MASS. DEC. 22nd 1620.

REESE

The tickets were beast and all, but it wasn't even about that with me. I just wanted to win. Because I'm a really competitive person. Ask anybody on my soccer team—I get fired up just for scrimmages!

And there just aren't a ton of chances to pwn the whole school in something.

actually a word (go figure)

Except for Battle of the Books. Which
is seriously unfair. 'Cause the only way
you can win that is to, like, y'know...

CLAUDIA

Read books?

REESE

Yeah. So that's not a good situation for
me. But a scavenger hunt? Totally my thing.

CLAUDIA

Scavenger Hunt Fever blew up so huge
that it even infected the Fembots.

I should explain about the Fembots.

Actually, no. I shouldn't. Because
as sixth grade president, it's my job to
represent everyone in our grade fairly and
equally. Even Fembots.

It would be VERY unpresidential of me
to badmouth anybody.

So I'm going to let Sophie do it.

SOPHIE

Okay, so it's basically like...if Satan
and the absolutely worst woman on *Violent*

Housewives had a baby, it'd be a Fembot. They're this group of girls at Culvert who are either crazy rich and think they're all that, like Athena Cohen and Ling Chen. Or they're total wannabes, like Meredith and Clarissa.

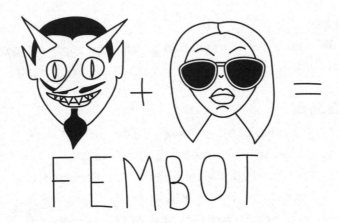

FEMBOT

CARMEN

I don't think the Fembots even cared about the tickets. I mean, Athena's dad can practically BUY Madison Square Garden. I think they just didn't like the idea that something might happen at Culvert that wasn't all about them.

Or maybe it was because all the cute seventh grade boys were doing it.

CLAUDIA

Whatever it was, the day after we announced the tickets, Parvati and I were talking in English class about whether I should try to be in the scavenger hunt.

It was a tough call, because I was totally desperate to see Miranda Fleet from the front row—but Akash and I were about to start putting the list of items together. And I knew it'd be totally unfair if I was the person who both made up the list AND searched for the things on it.

I was asking Parvati what she thought I should do, and Athena Cohen overheard us. She turned around in her chair and said in this incredibly snotty voice, "Do you ACTUALLY THINK you have a prayer of winning those tickets? What are you going to do— ride around Manhattan on your little pink scooters?"

PARVATI

That was SO ridiculous. We haven't ridden those scooters since, like, third grade.

little pink scooter
(had to take out of storage
for pic b/c I have not ridden
in YEARS)

CLAUDIA

But that's typical Athena. Mentioning them was her way of saying, "You are little peasants who have to ride around on scooters, and I am fabulously wealthy and own my own jet."

PARVATI

So I was all, "What are you going to do, Athena—have your butler carry you around on his shoulders?"

And she, like, curled her lip and went, "Whatever it takes, Poverty."

I swear she actually pronounced it that way—like, "Poverty" instead of "Parvati."

CLAUDIA

I know. I was there. It was beyond vile.

PARVATI

And I turned to you, and I was all, "OMG, Claude—you HAVE to be on our team. Because NOW IT'S PERSONAL."

CLAUDIA

I could not have agreed more.

So I went to Mrs. Bevan, and she said as long as I resigned from the Scavenger Hunt Committee before we started making up the list, it'd be fine.

So I formally stepped down as co-chair and devoted all my attention to building a team awesome enough to beat the Fembots and win the whole thing.

Which turned out to be kind of a major headache.

CHAPTER 5
WE ASSEMBLE AN
AWESOME TEAM
(AFTER A SLIGHTLY
HUGE ARGUMENT)

argument

team

CLAUDIA

It was Akash's idea for the scavenger hunt to have four-person teams. This seemed perfect, because it meant me, Sophie, Parvati, and Carmen could be one team—which we called Team Melting Pot on account of our ethnic diversity.

Asian American
Indian American
Cuban American
Miscellaneous American (me)

But unfortunately, the scavenger hunt was on a Saturday. And on Saturdays, Sophie is way overscheduled.

SOPHIE

I have ballet from 9 to 11 and conversational Korean from 2 to 4. But that wasn't even the problem. The problem was I had a violin recital that day. And there was, like, no way I could skip it. I've been practicing the Concerto in G FOR-E-VER.

CLAUDIA

I could totally respect that, even though I was very sad. Not only because Sophie would've been a huge asset, but also because she's my best friend on the planet.

So we needed a fourth person for Melting Pot. And Carmen, Parvati, and I had a real difference of opinion about who it should be.

Personally, I thought we should look for someone with skills we didn't have. For example, it seemed like a good idea to recruit a boy in case we had to find boy-specific stuff.

comic books
Pokémon cards
anything gross
etc.

And I thought a sporty, athletic boy would be particularly good, because Parvati and Carmen and I are more indoor types.

Plus, it seemed like since we were all Americans, it'd be smart to get someone who was foreign-born, just in case we needed an "outsider's perspective."

And when I added all that up, Jens Kuypers was a no-brainer, because he is A) a boy, B) very athletic, and C) just moved here from the Netherlands last summer.

Netherlands = Dutch tiny/cute country (with windmills)

PARVATI

I'm sorry, but can we just be honest here? The ONLY reason you wanted Jens on the team is because D) HE'S YOUR BOYFRIEND.

CARMEN

Seriously, Claudia. You totally jammed us with your Dutch boy toy.

CLAUDIA

I am just going to address this

issue head-on and be completely honest about it.

First of all, Jens is NOT technically my boyfriend. Mostly because I don't think "boyfriend"/"girlfriend" should apply to sixth graders. That's more of a seventh-grade-and-up situation.

Although it is true Jens and I are going out. I'm not going to get into details about our relationship, because it's nobody's business. But I will say it's been almost two and a half weeks so far, and it is going great.

However, that is ABSOLUTELY NOT why I wanted Jens on our team. I sincerely thought that when it came to beating the Fembots, he'd be more strategically helpful than Parvati and Carmen's first choice, Kalisha Hendricks.

PARVATI

And I was like, "THAT IS RIDICULOUS."

Because Jens is cute and friendly and all? But, no offense? He always seemed kind of lazy to me.

And I'm sorry, but Kalisha is brilliant.

CARMEN

She is SO brilliant! She's the smartest person in our class!

CLAUDIA

I don't know about THAT. I mean, yes, Kalisha's brilliant. No question.

But there are a LOT of smart people in our class. For example, that math test last week? Kalisha only got a 94. And I know for a fact that at LEAST one other person got a 96.

PARVATI

Who? You?

CLAUDIA

It's not important who it was. I'm just saying.

And again—Jens was bringing boy-specific knowledge we didn't have—

PARVATI

So was Kalisha! Because she lives in Queens! Which, like, NOBODY who doesn't live there knows anything about.

I mean, seriously. I'm not even sure where Queens is.

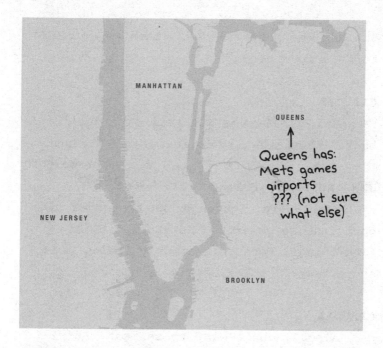

CARMEN

    Kalisha would've been SO helpful. AND she was psyched to be on our team.

CLAUDIA

    For the record, I'd like to point out that Kalisha was also totally fine with NOT being on our team.

KALISHA HENDRICKS, one of the smartest *(but not necessarily THE smartest)* ↰
kids in our class

It was all good. I just hooked up with Yun and Charlotte instead. Then we got Max to be a fourth.

CLAUDIA

And FYI, Jens is NOT lazy. He's just laid-back. AND he was very motivated to kick butt.

JENS KUYPERS, friend *NOT technically a boyfriend (see pp. 28—29)*

Yeah, sure. Scavenger hunt sounded like good fun. To go around New York City and find things, because I am only living here a short time, I think, "This is cool to do."

CLAUDIA

Also, I don't want to be mean, but I think Jens appreciated being rescued from playing on a team that, tbh, had absolutely no chance of winning.

Of course, my brother didn't see it that way.

REESE

I could NOT believe my sister stole Jens from us! I worked 24/7 putting Beast

Squad together! Me, Xander, Wyatt, and Jens
would've been a dream team!

In fact, we almost called ourselves
Dream Team instead of Beast Squad.

CLAUDIA

Again, not trying to be mean here. But
Dream Team would've been a MUCH better name,
because Reese was dreaming to think he had a
snowball's chance of winning.

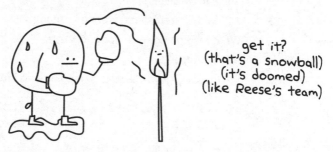

get it?
(that's a snowball)
(it's doomed)
(like Reese's team)

Basically, all the things Reese and
his friends are good at—like bouncing
soccer balls off their heads, or belching
the alphabet, or having wrestling matches in
our living room and breaking the furniture—
are totally useless in a scavenger hunt.

(actually
happened
TWICE)

But that didn't stop them from
completely freaking out when Jens joined
Melting Pot. Check out this exchange I
found on Jens's ClickChat wall:

CLICKCHAT POSTS ON JENS KUYPERS'S PUBLIC WALL

Xander — XlzKillinIt YO JK WUT DIS ISH BOUT U DMPNG US FR GIRLZ?

Jens — kuypersjens what does this mean?

XlzKillinIt REESE SEZ U PUNKIN TRUE DAT?

kuypersjens I am sorry Xander I do not understand your English

Reese — SKRONKMONSTER Are you srsly on my sisterz team for scavenger hunt?

kuypersjens oh yes guys sorry

XlzKillinIt !!!!!!!!JUDAS!!!!!!!!!

SKRONKMONSTER You said u were on r team!

Wyatt — killrkickr What r we going to do for a forth?

XlzKillinIt NOT KEWL YO

kuypersjens Im sorry guys Claudia is my girlfriend I must go with her

↖ technically we are JUST GOING OUT (Jens's English = not perfect)

REESE

I was seriously ripped when Jens quit. But then I was like, "It's cool. We'll just be a three-man. We're STILL going to pwn it!"

CLAUDIA

Unfortunately for Beast Squad, two days before the hunt, Mrs. Bevan told them that since they had an extra spot, she was adding James Mantolini to their team.

I should explain about James Mantolini.

Actually, no. I should let Reese do it.

REESE

I don't like to trash-talk people. But there's something seriously wrong with James Mantolini.

It's hard to explain. It's like Earth isn't his home planet or something.

Like, if you said, "Hey, James, what's two plus two?" He'd be like, "Sausages!"

And he gets in a LOT of trouble at school. He's always been like that. Back in kindergarten, he got sent to the principal's office for eating Molly Preston's hair. While it was still attached to her head.

It was pretty nuts. I was sitting next to Molly when it happened, and I'm, like, NEVER going to be able to get that image out of my mind.

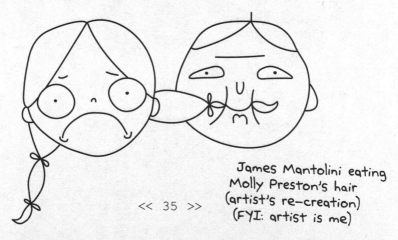

James Mantolini eating
Molly Preston's hair
(artist's re-creation)
(FYI: artist is me)

So it wasn't a surprise nobody wanted
James on their team. And when Mrs. Bevan put
him on Beast Squad, Xander and Wyatt and I
got pretty skreeved.

N.A.A.W.
("Not An
Actual
Word")

I'm not saying EVERYTHING crazy and
illegal that happened was because of James.

But at least half of it was.

The other half was Dad's fault.

CHAPTER 6
THE CHAPERONE
SITUATION

CLAUDIA

As sixth grade class president, I am fully aware that leadership is about responsibility. When something goes wrong, a true leader has to step up and take their share of the blame.

But the chaperone situation was totally not my fault.

Because it wasn't until three days before the hunt that Mrs. Bevan suddenly decided every team needed one. So Akash and I had to find 25 parent volunteers on seriously short notice. And we wound up with some not-great candidates.

Like my dad.

Dad's a lawyer, and here's the thing about lawyers: they're usually working on Saturdays. And Sundays. And pretty much every other day. And night. (plus holidays / vacations / birthdays / etc.)

I will say that even though he works crazy hours, Dad cares about us a lot. Which is why he wound up agreeing to chaperone with only minor guilt-tripping from Mom:

MOM AND DAD (text messages)

you need to chaperone Reese's team in scav hunt this Sat 10-4

Can you do it? Getting crushed this week

I am already chaperoning Claudia's team

Can they be on same team?

Have you met our children?

Fine. But might need to bring laptop and work while I'm there

Oh, sure. That's not unrealistic at all

Are you being sarcastic?

Very.

BUT I LOVE YOU

> Love you, too! Should I pick up dinner on way home?

It's midnight. I ate hours ago. Going to bed

> OMG. I need a new job

You really do

CLAUDIA

Incidentally, Dad also got stuck bankrolling Reese's entire pledge sheet.

REESE

I totally meant to get a whole ton of pledges. But I had soccer practice the day they handed the sheets out, and my pledge sheet wound up in the bottom of my backpack under my cleats.

And then I just kind of forgot it was there until, like, ten minutes before the hunt.

other things Reese has forgotten/ lost in bottom of backpack:
—report card
—field trip permission slip
—dirty socks (very smelly)
—week-old sandwich (very VERY smelly)

CLAUDIA

For the historical record, here's what Reese's sheet looked like:

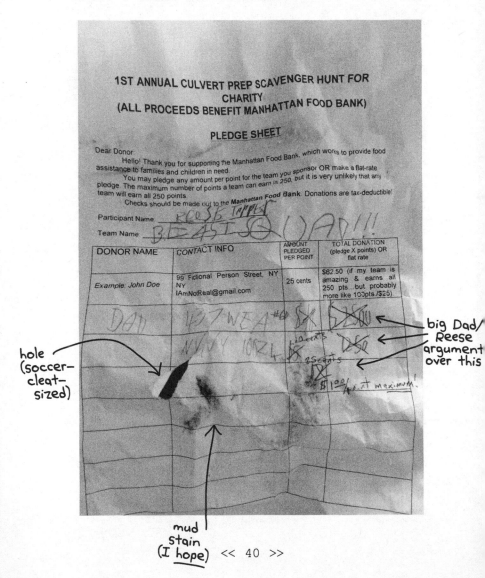

Not to brag or anything, but here's what MY sheet looked like:

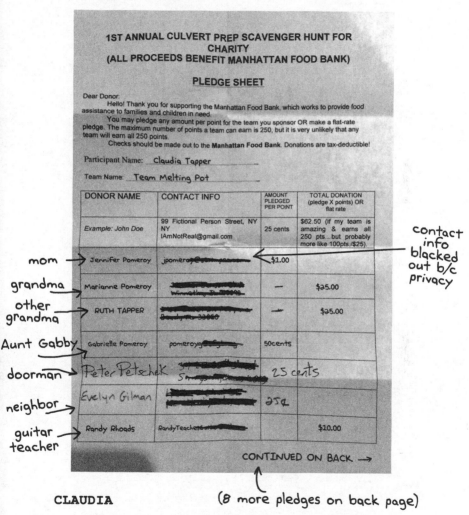

**1ST ANNUAL CULVERT PREP SCAVENGER HUNT FOR CHARITY
(ALL PROCEEDS BENEFIT MANHATTAN FOOD BANK)**

PLEDGE SHEET

Dear Donor:
    Hello! Thank you for supporting the Manhattan Food Bank, which works to provide food assistance to families and children in need.
    You may pledge any amount per point for the team you sponsor OR make a flat-rate pledge. The maximum number of points a team can earn is 250, but it is very unlikely that any team will earn all 250 points.
    Checks should be made out to the **Manhattan Food Bank**. Donations are tax-deductible!

Participant Name: _Claudia Tapper_

Team Name: _Team Melting Pot_

DONOR NAME	CONTACT INFO	AMOUNT PLEDGED PER POINT	TOTAL DONATION (pledge X points) OR flat rate
Example: John Doe	99 Fictional Person Street, NY NY IAmNotReal@gmail.com	25 cents	$62.50 (if my team is amazing & earns all 250 pts...but probably more like 100pts./$25).
Jennifer Pomeroy	jpomer~~@~~	$1.00	
Marianne Pomeroy	~~blacked out~~	—	$25.00
RUTH TAPPER	~~blacked out~~	—	$25.00
Gabrielle Pomeroy	pomeroy~~@~~	50cents	
Peter Petschek	~~blacked out~~	25 cents	
Evelyn Gilman	~~blacked out~~	25¢	
Randy Rhoads	RandyTeaches~~@~~		$10.00

mom → (Jennifer Pomeroy)

grandma → (Marianne Pomeroy)

other grandma → (RUTH TAPPER)

Aunt Gabby → (Gabrielle Pomeroy)

doorman → (Peter Petschek)

neighbor → (Evelyn Gilman)

guitar teacher → (Randy Rhoads)

contact info blacked out b/c privacy

CONTINUED ON BACK →

(8 more pledges on back page)

CLAUDIA

At first, it was not obvious Dad was

going to be a problem. In fact, on the morning of the hunt, I was much more worried about Mom.

The night before, we'd all agreed that since I was supposed to be at school by 9:00 to help Akash and Mrs. Bevan set up, our whole family would leave the house together at 8:45.

By 8:41, I was standing at the front door of our apartment, all ready to go.

At 8:50, I was STILL standing at the front door. And I was getting very, very mad at my whole family.

Mom was drying her hair. Reese was still in his underwear. And Dad had just gotten a phone call from somebody at work named Larry.

I knew this because Dad kept yelling things into the phone like, "Larry, it's doable..." And "Larry! We'll deal with it...!" And "LARRY! QUIT FREAKING OUT! THIS IS NOT A CRISIS!"

Which was weird, because A) Dad seemed like HE was the one freaking out, and B) it actually did sound like a crisis.

By 8:53, Mom was finally ready, so we left Dad and Reese behind and headed to school.

REESE

That was totally uncool to leave without us. I was ready to go!

CLAUDIA

Are you crazy? You weren't even wearing pants.

REESE

I could've put them on in the elevator.

CLAUDIA

I am not even going to bother explaining why that's a bad idea.

building elevator—
NOT OKAY
to be in here
without pants

So Mom and I got a cab on West End Avenue, and as we started across town, Mom said, "This should be a fun day.... I'm looking forward to meeting Jens."

This is the point where I realized having my mom chaperone a team that included the boy I was going out with might end up being the worst mistake of my life.

We spent the rest of the cab ride working out the ground rules for any Mom-Jens interaction. By the time we got to Culvert Prep, Mom had agreed to act like she had no idea Jens and I were going out, *mostly unwritten rules (b/c no time to write them down) (also v. hard to write in back of cab)* pretend she'd never heard his name before, and only ask him the kind of questions you'd ask someone if you were just being polite.

We also settled on a code word that I could use if she was saying or doing something embarrassing and I needed her to stop right away: "lip balm."

good for chapped lips and/or code word

As we got out of the cab, I realized
the code word might be a problem if I
actually needed to borrow Mom's lip balm for
real.

But then I saw the Mysterious Black Car
in front of the school, and I totally forgot
about the lip balm and everything else.

if this were a movie,
OMINOUS BLACK CAR MUSIC
would start here

CHAPTER 7
THE MYSTERIOUS
BLACK CAR

CLAUDIA

It was one of those car-service-type cars, with tinted windows and a personal driver. And it was just sitting there at the curb, like it was waiting to chauffeur somebody's team around the city all day.

MYSTERIOUS BLACK CAR (not actual car) (but looked like this) (except with tinted windows)

Which seemed like a MAJOR cheat.

Except it wouldn't technically be cheating...UNLESS there was enough time to add "NO CARS" to the list of rules.

So I ran into the auditorium to talk over
a last-minute rule change with Akash and
Mrs. Bevan.

But I couldn't get their attention,
because they were having a gigantic fight.

AKASH

It was ridiculous! The Brooklyn Bridge
thing was the coolest item on the whole
list! And she made me take it out! For a
COMPLETELY stupid reason!

CLAUDIA

I was on Mrs. Bevan's side with that
one. Trying to get that Brooklyn Bridge item
actually WOULD have been life-threatening.

AKASH

No kidding! THAT'S WHY IT WAS WORTH
TWENTY POINTS!

CLAUDIA

But scavenger hunts aren't supposed to
be deadly.

AKASH

THE FUN ONES ARE! It was like my worst

nightmare! I created a masterpiece, and Mrs. Bevan ruined it with her lame rules! I seriously considered resigning in protest.

CLAUDIA

After Akash finally agreed not to quit and go home, I asked about adding a no-car rule. But Mrs. Bevan was too stressed out over having to black out the Brooklyn Bridge line from everybody's list of items to deal with anything else.

People were starting to show up by then, and each team got an envelope with **"DO NOT OPEN"** printed on the front, a rule sheet, and a Calvin the Cat.

CALVIN THE CATS

Calvin's our school mascot, and the cats were the same little stuffed ones that Culvert Prep hands out to kids on the first day of kindergarten. At first, I wasn't sure why every team was getting one.

AKASH

Half the list was photos, and we had to make sure they were all taken during the hunt. So we decided to give everybody an object they had to include in each shot.

And I had some AWESOME ideas for the object. But they all cost money. So Mrs. Bevan made me use the stupid Calvins, because she had a whole pile of them sitting in a closet. And she's a complete you-know-what.

← (cheapskate)

(Sorry again, Akash)

CLAUDIA

The Calvins definitely confused people. When I walked out of the auditorium to look for the rest of my team, I saw my brother's idiot friend Xander throw Beast Squad's Calvin into a garbage can.

XANDER

I's all, "WUUUT? This ain't no first day of kindergarten, yo."

CLAUDIA

I was about to point out to Xander that there was probably a scavenger-hunt-related reason for the Calvins when Parvati and Carmen showed up.

They were freaking out. Parvati practically screamed, "DID YOU SEE ALL THE TOWN CARS?"

Right away, I got scared. Because I'd only seen one car.

PARVATI

I was like, "OMG, Claude: THERE'S FOUR OF THEM!!!"

CLAUDIA

All I could think was, "If FOUR different teams are getting chauffeured around the city...we are doomed."

CARMEN

I was trying to get you guys to chill. Because on a bad traffic day—like, if there's a parade, or a bunch of street fairs—it's actually faster to take the subway. So having a car service might not be that huge an advantage.

CLAUDIA

The three of us sat down and tried to figure out which teams were rich and obnoxious enough to pay for a car service for all six hours of the hunt.

The Fembots—who were calling themselves Goddesses, Inc., even though a better name would've been The Brides of Satan—were a no-brainer.

But except for a couple of no-way-they'd-do-that teams, like the Avada Kedavras, *← Kalisha's team* pretty much everybody was a possible suspect.

We were going down the list when Jens arrived. He asked what we were talking about, and when we told him, he said, "Don't we just go by walking?"

Most likely car service users:
—The Fierceness
—Cutsies!
—Gingivitis
—Knights Who Say Ni
—Fire Team Four
—Killaz
—The Wut Ups

He got a little side-eye from Carmen and Parvati for that.

CARMEN

I was like, "Hello? Manhattan is TWELVE MILES LONG."

← actually 13.4 miles (but close enough)

JENS

I said to Carmen, "But weather is beautiful today! Perfect for a walk."

↑
tbh, weather actually WAS beautiful

PARVATI

I'm not going to lie. I was ALL kinds of worried about Jens with that attitude. He was like, "Oh, let's just wander around and sniff some flowers."

And I was like, "Excuse me, but we are in a FIGHT TO THE DEATH here? And the Fembots are using a car service? And so are three other teams? Soooo this is kind of a crisis?"

CLAUDIA

I was about to take Jens aside and remind him how important winning was to the rest of Team Melting Pot, but just then Mom came up to us. I braced myself for some Mom-Jens awkwardness, but she didn't even look at him.

Instead, in a very stressed-out voice, she said, "Have you seen your brother?"

I had not. Probably because right that minute, he and Dad were running full speed down 77th Street.

CHAPTER 8
REESE AND DAD
ALMOST MISS
THE WHOLE THING

REESE

After I got my pants on, Dad was still
on his work call. So I sat down to play some
MetaWorld and then just kind of spaced on
the time until Wyatt texted me and was like,
"WHERE ARE YOU?"

And I realized it was, like, five
minutes to ten.

So I went into panic mode. And I
got Dad off his call—which was TOTALLY
stressing him out—and we, like, ska-jammed
downstairs and into a cab.

N.A.A.W.

In the cab, Dad checked a work
email on his phone and then made this
"muuuugh" noise, like somebody slugged
him in the gut.

Then he looked at me and went, "Let
me ask you something, kiddo..." in that
really quiet voice he uses when, like, your
goldfish just died and he has to flush it
down the toilet.

only known photo
of Reese's goldfish
"Swimmy"
(lived 3 days)

So I knew what was coming couldn't be good.

And Dad was like, "How badly do you need a chaperone?"

And I was like, "Dad—you TOTALLY can't bail on us."

Then the cab got stuck in traffic and we had to jump out and start running.

MOM AND DAD (text messages)

Have you left yet? 10 min till start

5 min till start

Please tell me you are en route and not still on phone

3 min till start

WHERE ARE YOU???

<< 54 >>

ERIC????!!!!!

IT'S STARTING NOW

rubbing

WHAT?!

running

HURRY!

CLAUDIA

Mrs. Bevan gave an intro speech
thanking everybody for coming, and reminding
us this was for charity, and we were all
winners just for showing up to support the
Manhattan Food Bank, so we shouldn't get too
competitive.

Which everybody ignored, because the
whole auditorium was thinking, "FRONT-ROW
SEATS AT THE GARDEN! I'LL STEP OVER DEAD
BODIES TO WIN THIS!"

Then she went over the rules. For the
historical record—and because certain rules
turned out to be VERY important—here's what
the rule sheet looked like:

1ST ANNUAL CULVERT PREP MIDDLE SCHOOL SCAVENGER HUNT FOR CHARITY

<u>RULES</u>

OBJECTIVE: To earn the most points by collecting as many of the items on the list as possible. Please note: <u>different items have different point values</u>.

TEAMS: Each team has a maximum of four members. Team members should remain together during the hunt.

CHAPERONES: Each team must have an adult chaperone at all times.

CHEATING: All items/photos must be acquired DURING the hunt, by team members only. Any team found breaking this rule will be disqualified.

PHOTOS: All photos MUST include Calvin the Cat to receive full points.

CHECK-IN: Each team should check in on the official scavenger hunt Clickchat wall (@CzarOfTheHunt) at least once per hour.

TIME LIMIT: The hunt ends at 4:00PM SHARP. Your entire team MUST be present with their items in the Culvert Prep auditorium by this time. Latecomers will be disqualified.

PRIZES: **FIRST PRIZE:** four (4) front-row tickets to ANY EVENT at Madison Square Garden between now and the last day of school (June 14).
SECOND PRIZE: One (1) $20 Starbucks gift card, to be shared equally by all four team members.
THIRD PRIZE: Four (4) Culvert Prep pencil cases.
FOURTH PRIZE: There is no fourth prize.

EMERGENCIES, ETC: Serious problems, call/text Mrs. Bevan: ▬▬▬▬▬▬
Non-serious problems, message Akash G. on ClickChat (@CzarOfTheHunt)

PLEDGES: Please turn all pledge money in to Mrs. Bevan's office by close of school <u>Monday, Nov. 3</u>. Make checks payable to Manhattan Food Bank.

CLAUDIA

    After she went over the rules, Mrs. Bevan asked if there were any questions.

Figuring we were finally getting started, the whole auditorium got halfway out of their seats—but then Dimitri Sharansky's mom raised her hand and asked if all the items on the list were nut-free.

Which took forever for Mrs. Bevan to answer, because she had to google some things on her phone. And everybody got really annoyed at Dimitri's mom.
Especially Dimitri (even though his nut allergy is actually very serious).

potentially fatal to Dimitri Sharansky

At some point in the middle of that, Reese and Dad showed up.

REESE

It was seriously confusing. We ran in, all out of breath and sweaty—and the whole auditorium was, like, watching Mrs. Bevan stare at her phone.

CLAUDIA

Finally, Mrs. Bevan said, "Yes! Everything's nut-free. Any other questions...? No? Then LET THE HUNT BEGIN!"

There was a ripping noise as everybody opened their envelopes, and we all got our first look at the list:

1ST ANNUAL CULVERT PREP SCAVENGER HUNT FOR CHARITY
LIST OF ITEMS
ALL PHOTOS <u>MUST HAVE</u> A STUFFED CALVIN THE CAT IN THEM!!!

bookmark from The Strand Bookstore (Greenwich Village) – 3 points
photo of Wall Street Charging Bull statue (Financial District)– 3 pts.
bottle cap from 5-cent Coke machine at Tekserve (Chelsea) – 3 pts
bamboo back scratcher from Ting's (Chinatown) – 3 pts
photo of Imagine mosaic in Strawberry Fields (Central Park) – 3 pts
Metro North Harlem Line train schedule (Grand Central) – 3 pts
napkin with Waldorf Astoria hotel logo (Upper East Side) – 3 pts
pizza menu showing a slice for 99 cents or less – 4 pts
bag of fake cat poop from New York Costumes (Greenwich Village) – 4 pts
visitor's map of Natural History Museum (Upper West Side) – 4 pts
three buttered popcorn jelly beans from Dylan's Candy Bar (Upper East
        Side) – 4 pts
shopping bag from Forbidden Planet (Greenwich Village) – 4 pts
tiny (3-inch or smaller) statue of Empire State Building (Midtown) – 5 pts
Playbill from a Broadway musical (Times Square) – 5 pts
customer ticket from Katz's Deli (Lower East Side) – 5 pts
taxi cab receipt for a trip over 1 mile – 5 pts
order card from Nom Wah Tea Parlor (Chinatown) – 5 pts
photo of India's national flag in front of United Nations (Midtown) – 6 pts
handbill from a solo artist show at a Chelsea art gallery (Chelsea) – 6 pts
photo of a painting with a dog in it from Metropolitan Museum of Art (Upper
        East Side) – 6 pts
photo of Bethesda Fountain taken from middle of rowboat pond (Central
        Park) – 7 pts
one cannoli from Caffe Palermo (Little Italy) – 8 pts
handbill of upcoming shows at the Apollo Theater (Harlem) – 8 pts
photo of price tag for item over $100,000 at Bloomingdale's (Upper East
        Side) – 8 pts
postcard from Roosevelt Island Visitor's Center (Roosevelt Island) – 8 pts
photo of guy in Flubby suit holding Calvin the Cat (Times Square) – 8 pts
photo of Yankee Stadium Gate 4 (Bronx) – 10 pts
video of 1st 4 notes of Beethoven's 5th symphony, played on FAO
        Schwarz floor piano (Midtown) – 10 pts
photo of Statue of Liberty taken from deck of Staten Island ferry (Hudson
        River) – 10 pts
photo of dog walker with at least 4 dogs on leash – 12 pts (+2 pts for
        each additional dog)
photo of World's Fair Unisphere (Queens) – 12 pts
photo taken from front car of Coney Island Cyclone (Brooklyn) – 15 pts

one Cronut from Dominique Ansel bakery (SoHo) – 30 pts
photo of Calvin the Cat getting kissed by Deondra – 500 pts

used to be
Brooklyn
Bridge item

<< 58 >>

AKASH

Even without the Brooklyn Bridge thing, that list was a masterpiece.

CLAUDIA

Except for that one giant mistake that wound up having terrible consequences for everybody.

AKASH

It's not my fault people can't take a joke.

CLAUDIA

There were a few seconds of quiet while people scanned the list. Then there was a mad rush for the exit.

We hit the sidewalk, and the first thing I saw was Meredith Timms getting into one of the car service cars as a driver in a suit held her door open.

Then Ling Chen, getting into the second car...

Followed by Clarissa Parker, disappearing into the third one...

And finally Athena Cohen and her mom, headed for the last one.

All four Fembots. In four different
cars.

CARMEN

I practically had a heart attack.

PARVATI

I think I might have, like, screamed or
something.

artist's re-creation of
Parvati after seeing
Fembots drive off in
four different cars
(Parvati does NOT
look like this)
(if confused, google
"The Scream painting")

CLAUDIA

It was more of a yelp. But yeah. You did.
Which was totally understandable.
Because the hunt was only two minutes old—
and already, the Fembots were crushing us.

CHAPTER 9
MY BROTHER'S
TEAM IS WEIRD
AND DISGUSTING

CLAUDIA

I am going to let Reese explain what happened with Beast Squad, because A) I wasn't there, and B) I still don't even understand half of it. It was all way too random.

REESE

When Mrs. Bevan set everybody loose, Xander and Wyatt ran over to us, and Wyatt was like, "Xander threw away our Calvin!"

Dad and I were like, "Whaaa?" We'd just gotten there, so we didn't even know all the teams had gotten a Calvin to use in pictures.

Xander was like, "Yo, I got this." Then he went over to this garbage can and practically dove in.

And I was like, "Are we hunting for things in garbage cans? 'Cause that's kinda skreevy."

N.A.A.W.

WYATT

Then James Mantolini showed up. And he was like, "Let's get ready to rumble."

Except he said it in this really creepy voice, like he was talking in a foreign accent. So it was more like, "Lheeets gheet rheeedy to rhuuuuum-bal." James is so weird.

REESE

Then Xander popped up out of the garbage can, going, "YO, DAWG, THAT IS NASTY!"

XANDER

Some fool straight-up bombed that can with a gallon of Starbucks. So when I peeped dem cat, it was like some kinda wet, hot coffee sponge.

WYATT

It was pretty gross. The Calvin was, like, dripping hot coffee.

And we were like, "What are we going to do?"

And James was like, "Let's take a picture—maybe it's under warranty."

REESE

And I was all, "Dude—how is that helpful? We need it fixed, like, NOW."

So James goes, "Fine. I'll suck the coffee out."

JAMES MANTOLINI, Beast Squad member/very strange person

I was being a friend of the earth. You know: recycling the coffee.

REESE

So James, like, shoved the whole head in his mouth. And he basically gagged on it and started to choke—

Beast Squad's Calvin post-coffee (also post-James's mouth) (eeeew)

CLAUDIA

I'm sorry. I hate to interrupt. Can you skip ahead to a non-disgusting part?

REESE

Sorry. So eventually, James quit choking to death, and we wrung most of the coffee out of the Calvin. But it was still all brown and soggy—

CLAUDIA

Seriously. Skip ahead.

REESE

Okay! Geez.

So we checked out the list, and we saw all the high-point stuff was at the bottom. So we figured the smart thing was to start there and work our way up.

The first thing was 500 points for a pic of Calvin getting kissed by Deondra.

one Cronut from Dominique Ansel bakery (SoHo) – 30 pts
photo of Calvin the Cat getting kissed by Deondra – 500 pts

Akash was still inside the auditorium, so I poked my head back in and yelled, "HEY,

AKASH! IS THAT DEONDRA THING A JOKE?"

And Akash was like, "OF COURSE IT'S A
JOKE!!!"

WYATT

Then I said, "It's 500 points if we get
it, though, right?"

And Akash was like, "Oh, sure! Just
track down the most famous pop star in the
universe by four o'clock and get her to
kiss your little stuffed animal, and you're
golden."

I think he was being sarcastic. But I
would've tried to do it if our Calvin hadn't
just been in James's mouth. And also the
garbage. So I didn't think Deondra would be
up for kissing it even if we could find her.

REESE

The next-biggest thing on the list was
30 points for a "Cronut."

So I yelled, "HEY, AKASH! WHAT'S A
CRONUT?"

And he yelled back, "STOP ASKING ME
QUESTIONS!"

And Xander was like, "Cronut, yo!
That's my jam!"

XANDER

Dem Cronuts iz BEAST! Straight up. Like heaven in yo' mouth.

REESE

Here's the thing I learned about Cronuts: they're incredibly delicious. But there's only one bakery in the city that sells them. And they only make a few every day. So people get up early and stand in line for, like, HOURS to buy them.

XANDER

True dat. When I gots da Cronut itch? Mom-a-saurus pays our dog walker fiddy bones to get up crack-o'-dawn and represent on dat line to get one in my belly.

REESE

Your mom pays a guy fifty bucks to get you a Cronut? Wow. That's pretty nuts.

XANDER

Troof! Momma loves her X-Man.

this might explain why
Xander is so horrible
(VERY bad parenting)

REESE

When Xander told us how hard the
Cronuts were to get, I started to think it
might not be worth the hassle. But then
Dad—who'd been standing off to one side,
typing emails on his phone—suddenly went,
"The Cronut bakery's in SoHo? LET'S GO!"

Before we knew it, he'd piled us all
into a minivan cab, and we were headed
downtown to SoHo.

Which just happened to be on the way to
Dad's office.

SoHo = "SOuth of
HOuston Street" =
lots of shopping
(and tourists)
(and close to
Dad's office)

CHAPTER 10
MY TEAM'S VERY BAD
(AND THEN VERY GOOD)
START

CLAUDIA

For Team Melting Pot, the first few
minutes were kind of a blur. There was a lot
of yelling and a lot of running, and it's
very hard to do both of those things at once.

We were yelling because everybody had
a different opinion about how to handle the
Fembots. Using four different cars seemed
totally illegal under the "team members
should remain together" rule.

TEAMS: Each team has a maximum of four members. Team members
should remain together during the hunt.

But we couldn't agree on whether to try
and bust them for it ourselves, or let some
other team rat them out to Mrs. Bevan.

And we were running because we knew we
had to move fast to have any prayer of winning
if the Fembots didn't get disqualified.

We were headed for the Met, because it
was the closest place to the school with a

high-point item (6 points, for a photo of a painting with a dog in it).

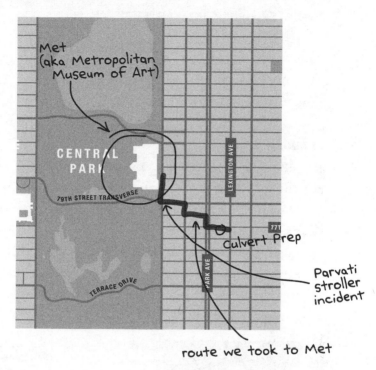

route we took to Met

PARVATI

I was all, "We HAVE to get the Fembots disqualified!"

And your mom was all, "Let's just run our own race and not worry about other teams."

And you were all, "Mom—LIP BALM!" Which was totally random.

code word did not work b/c Mom forgot what it was

CARMEN

And I was all, "WHY ISN'T YOUR SPORTY BOYFRIEND RUNNING FASTER?"

JENS

I did not think there was running. If I knew this, I would have worn other shoes.

CLAUDIA

Here's the thing: by 12-year-old-boy standards, Jens has AMAZING taste in clothes. This is normally awesome. But in terms of the hunt, it was kind of a problem. Because he was wearing these very cool blue-and-gray leather shoes that looked great with his outfit, but seemed like they were very hard to run in.

Jens's shoes = very cool (but NOT good for running)

So he was kind of slowing us down.

Although Parvati was ALSO slowing us down—because she was trying to dial Mrs. Bevan's phone number while running full speed down the sidewalk and yelling at us.

Which, BTW, made her kind of a menace. At one point, she almost plowed into a stroller and trampled a two-year-old and his nanny.

PARVATI

I'm sorry, but that nanny? NOT doing her job. She should've seen me coming and swerved out of the way.

But I got Mrs. Bevan on the phone. And she was all, "Thank you for the information. I will investigate."

Which was, like, NOT satisfying. So when we got to the museum, I decided to post on the scavenger hunt ClickChat wall to, like, publicly shame the Fembots.

CLAUDIA

The Met was packed with tourists, and the line to get a ticket was insane.

Met Museum: CRAZY busy on Saturdays

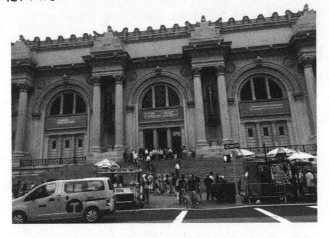

Fortunately, Carmen is very into art, so she has a Met membership, and the line for members was only one person long. Within a minute, Carmen was heading to one of the galleries with our Calvin the Cat to take a picture of a painting with a dog in it.

The rest of us sat on a bench in the lobby to wait for her. Right away, it got awkward with Mom and Jens. Mom started with, "So, we haven't been formally introduced...." And then she went right into, "You're new to Culvert? Where were you before...?" And "The NETHERLANDS! How great! What brought you to New York...?"

Jens is actually very polite and good

with adults, so I tried my best to ignore them while I monitored the scavenger hunt's ClickChat wall on my phone. Parvati had just outed the Fembots for cheating, and things were starting to heat up:

CLICKCHAT POSTS ON "CULVERT PREP SCAVENGER HUNT" WALL

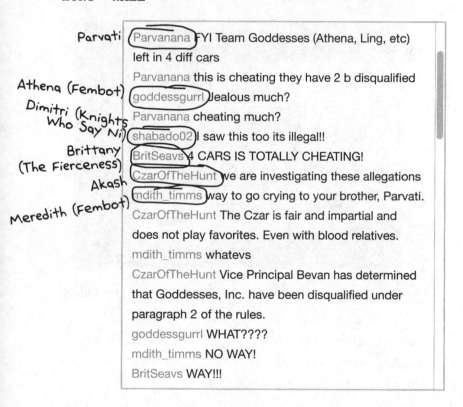

Parvati

Athena (Fembot)

Dimitri (Knights Who Say Ni)

Brittany (The Fierceness)

Akash

Meredith (Fembot)

Parvanana FYI Team Goddesses (Athena, Ling, etc) left in 4 diff cars

Parvanana this is cheating they have 2 b disqualified

goddessgurrl Jealous much?

Parvanana cheating much?

shabado02 I saw this too its illegal!!

BritSeavs 4 CARS IS TOTALLY CHEATING!

CzarOfTheHunt we are investigating these allegations

mdith_timms way to go crying to your brother, Parvati.

CzarOfTheHunt The Czar is fair and impartial and does not play favorites. Even with blood relatives.

mdith_timms whatevs

CzarOfTheHunt Vice Principal Bevan has determined that Goddesses, Inc. have been disqualified under paragraph 2 of the rules.

goddessgurrl WHAT????

mdith_timms NO WAY!

BritSeavs WAY!!!

CLAUDIA

When we saw Akash's message that the Fembots were disqualified, Parvati and I both screamed so loud we freaked out not only Mom and Jens, but a whole group of Japanese tourists.

Just then, Carmen showed up with the picture we needed.

dog

Calvin

CARMEN

I went straight to Early Modern Europe, because people were WAY into dogs back then. Like, you can't throw a rock in that gallery without hitting a dog picture.

CLAUDIA

We high-fived each other all the way
down the steps of the Met, then headed for
Central Park to get a couple more items. As
we walked into the park, I remember thinking
the Fembots' getting disqualified was too
good to be true.

Unfortunately, I was right.

CHAPTER 11
BLACK MARKET CRONUT

CLAUDIA

While Team Melting Pot was at the Met, Beast Squad was headed downtown to the Cronut bakery.

REESE

The whole way down to SoHo, Dad was up front in the passenger seat of the cab, typing work emails on his phone. Along the way, we passed the FAO Schwarz toy store, where there's this big floor piano you can play by jumping up and down on it.

We were like, "Let's stop and get the video of us playing Beethoven on the floor piano! It's worth ten points!"

FAO Schwarz floor piano

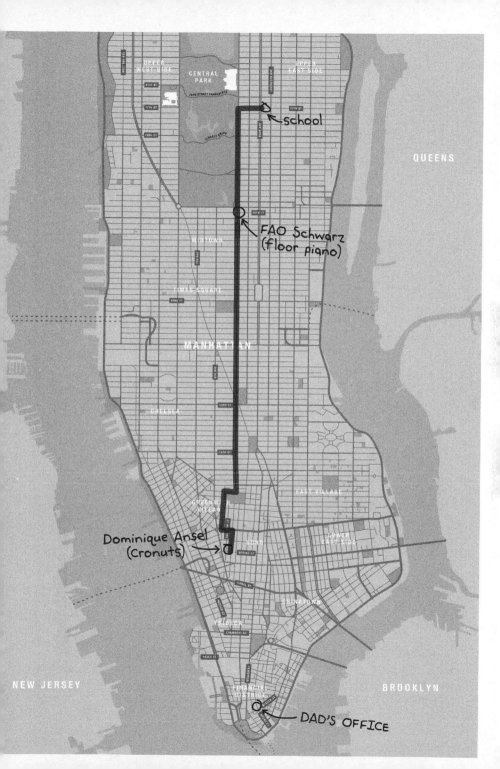

And Dad was like, "We'll get it later!
Let's go downtown!"

Which I guess was fine, because we
couldn't agree on what Beethoven's Fifth
Symphony sounded like.

First, I was like, "I know it! It's
dun-dun-DA-dun, dun, DA-DUN, dun DA-DUN."

WYATT

The rest of us were like, "Reese, dude:
that's the Darth Vader song."

But that got the Darth Vader song stuck
in everybody's head. So whenever somebody
tried to sing Beethoven's Fifth, it came out
sounding like Darth Vader.

REESE

By the time Wyatt googled the right
song on his phone—it's actually "dun-dun-
dun-DUN"—we were thirty
blocks past FAO Schwarz,
so it was too late
anyway.

But we did get five
points for "taxicab
receipt for trip over
1 mile."

When we got to the Cronut bakery, it *aka Dominique Ansel*
looked like we were in luck. Because when we
counted, there were only thirty-seven people
in line.

Cronut line

WYATT

But it turned out that was because they
were almost out of Cronuts. And when we got
in line, the people in front of us were all,
"Are you crazy? We've been here for hours! And
even WE probably aren't getting Cronuts!"

REESE

Then Dad was like, "Oh, well! Let's go

take a picture of the Wall Street bull statue!"

Which is, like, a block from Dad's office.

But I wasn't thinking of that. I was like, "Dad—the bull's only worth three points! A Cronut's worth THIRTY!"

Then all four of us started begging him to stay in line and give it a shot.

So Dad was like, "Let me do some investigating." He went up to the front of the store to check out the situation. The rest of us stayed at the back of the line, which was around the corner at the end of the block.

Wyatt got his phone out to check the scavenger hunt's ClickChat wall. There was some crazy stuff going on with Athena Cohen's team, so we started reading the messages.

WYATT

And that's when our Calvin got hit by a truck.

JAMES

It was Xander's fault.

> Xander's nickname for James (should be "J-Ma" or "J-Man," but Xander is idiot)
> ✓

XANDER

No way, dawg! That was ALL on J-Mo. Alls I did was smack him upside the head with the Calvin a coupla times.

J-Mo's the one who jacked it from me and drop-kicked it in the street right when the truck was going by.

WYATT

I actually heard a pop when its head exploded. That truck wheel caught it JUST right.

But the good thing was the stuffing was still all soggy from the coffee, so it didn't blow away. It just kind of oozed.

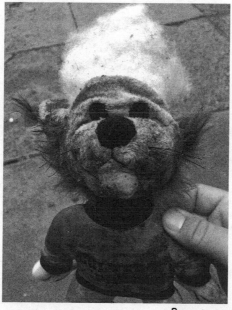

Beast Squad's Calvin
(after getting run over)

REESE

James was like, "Stand back! I'm a doctor!" And he tried to jam the stuffing back inside the Calvin's head. But there was no way to close it.

Wyatt and I were going to go buy some tape for the head, but then Dad came back.

And he was like, "I got bad news...and I got good news."

The bad news was the bakery had run out of Cronuts.

The good news was Dad had found a guy who'd just bought a Cronut and was willing to sell it to us.

But he wanted a CRAZY amount of money. Dad wouldn't tell us how much.

WYATT

I was like, "Is it more than fifty bucks?"

And your dad was like, "Yes."

And then I was like, "Is it more than a hundred?"

And he was like, "No comment."

REESE

Dad kind of lowered his voice and went,

"Here's the deal, guys: I'm willing to buy you
this Cronut. BUT...in return for that...
I need you to do me a VERY big favor."

Before he could tell us what the
favor was, this guy with a goatee came up
to him, holding a little yellow box from the
bakery.

little
yellow
box

And he was like, "Hey, buddy—are we
gonna do this? 'Cause otherwise, I'm eating
my Cronut."

And Dad looked at us and was like,
"Guys, do we have a deal? I get you the
Cronut, you do me a huge favor?"

XANDER

I's all, "HOOK US UP, babylicious!"

WYATT

I was a little worried. Not because of the money, or the favor thing, but because the guy selling the Cronut seemed kind of sketchy.

And then James yelled, "HOW MUCH DO YOU CHARGE FOR AN ASSASSINATION?" at him.

JAMES

All I'm saying is, anybody who sells black market Cronuts is probably doing a LOT of other stuff on the side. Like contract murders.

And I have some very powerful enemies I'd like to see neutralized.

CLAUDIA

Oh, really? Like who?

JAMES

I'll never tell. Because when it happens, my fingerprints can't be on it.

James is RIDICULOUS

REESE

So Xander put James in a headlock to get him to shut up long enough for Dad to pay the guy with the goatee some crazy

amount of money. Then the guy forked over
the box, and we sat down on a bench in this
little park by the bakery to open it up.

I was pretty curious, because until that
morning, I'd never even heard of a Cronut.

It was basically a fancy square-ish
donut with purple frosting.

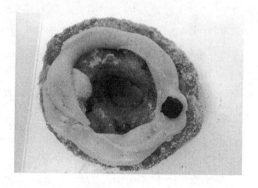

And then Xander went, "Yo, Homes—dat
ain't no Cronut!"

XANDER

Alls I know is, last time I had a
Cronut? That bad boy was chocolate. And this
was some kinda purple-fruity ish.

REESE

Dad was like, "Please tell me I did NOT
just buy a counterfeit Cronut."

And Wyatt was like, "Oh, yeah! It could totally be a fake!"

WYATT

It made sense. I mean, you can buy a Rolex watch in Chinatown for twenty bucks. But it's not really a Rolex.

And one time, my mom bought this, like, Louis Vuitton bag for $40 from some guy on the street? Only it was a total fake, and it fell apart in three days.

Mom doesn't really want me telling people that story. But it's true.

REESE

When Wyatt and Xander told him he'd paid a gazillion dollars for a fake Cronut, Dad basically turned white and looked like he was going to have a heart attack.

Then he took a picture of the Cronut and texted it to Mom.

MOM AND DAD (text messages)

> Does this look like a real Cronut?

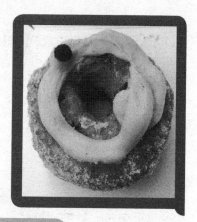

I don't even know what a Cronut is

V worried I just bought a fake

I have MUCH bigger problems right now. Have you seen the ClickChat page?

REESE

Eventually, Dad decided even if the Cronut was fake, the box looked real. So we should just turn it in and try to get our thirty points.

Then Dad was like, "Now, about that favor I need from you..."

And that's when the trouble started.

CHAPTER 12
ZOMBIE LAWYER FEMBOTS

BRAAAAAINS!

CLAUDIA

While Beast Squad's Calvin the Cat's head was exploding down in SoHo, so was mine.

Not literally. But almost literally.

Let me back up a little. After we left the museum, Team Melting Pot headed for the Central Park Boathouse to rent a boat and pick up 7 points for "photo of Bethesda Fountain from middle of rowboat pond."

But the line was RIDICULOUS.

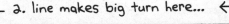

ROWBOAT RENTAL LINE

2. line makes big turn here...

3. line ends way down here at boathouse (not pictured)

1. line starts here...

CARMEN

I had no idea people were so into rowboats. That line was AT LEAST an hour long. I mean, there was no way we had time to stand in it.

But then Parvati had her brilliant idea.

PARVATI

It's not like the list said, "rent a rowboat." It just said, "take a picture from the rowboat pond."

So I was like, "Hel-lo? Let's just wade in and take the picture!"

CARMEN

And I was like, "THAT is gross." Because that pond water's green. And not healthy-natural green. More like incurable-diseases green. I was defs not stepping in it.

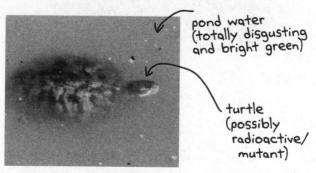

pond water (totally disgusting and bright green)

turtle (possibly radioactive/ mutant)

PARVATI

And I was like, "HEL-LO? That's why we have a boy on our team! To do the gross stuff!"

JENS

Parvati asked me to go in the water. But I said no. Because not good for my shoes.

PARVATI

I was like, "Seriously? TAKE YOUR SHOES OFF AND ROLL UP YOUR PANTS!"

JENS

I had bad pants for rolling. How do you say it? "Stovepipe"? Very hard to roll up.

Jens's pants
(v. stylish, but
def not good
for rolling up)

PARVATI

I seriously could not believe how useless Jens was. So I was like, "Fine. Whatevs. I'm going in."

CLAUDIA

Parvati ran to the pond, took off her shoes, rolled up her pants, and waded in with the Calvin in one hand and her phone in the other.

PARVATI

BTW, the thing I did NOT expect? Mud. The bottom of that pond is MAJOR sludge.

And your mom was all, "Parvati, this is NOT a good idea."

And then she was all, "POLICE COMING!"

CLAUDIA

It was just a park cop. But still. He was pointing at Parvati, yelling "HEY! GET OUTTA THERE!"

Carmen and I yelled, "TAKE THE PICTURE!" And Parvati got panicky and almost fell on her butt.

PARVATI

I totally freaked. I was like, "OMG, I am going to RUIN my phone. AND my whole outfit." But I didn't. And I got the shot!

Bethesda fountain

we were here (yelling)

park cop was here (also yelling)

disgusting pond water

Parvati was here (standing in pond water)

CLAUDIA

   I was very proud of Parvati for that.
And after she and my mom apologized to the
park cop, he let her off with a warning.

   Although, tbh, I think all park cops
can do is give warnings.

PARVATI

When I told my parents I went in the
rowboat pond, they made me get a tetanus shot.

But it was, like, SO worth it.

CLAUDIA

Parvati's getting that pic was the high
point of the morning. Because right after
that, things went downhill fast.

First, it took her forever (and about
1,000 hot dog napkins) to get the mud
off her feet. Then we went to Strawberry
Fields—which is a memorial to John Lennon
of the Beatles, who are the second-greatest
songwriters in history after Miranda Fleet—
and got a 3-point pic.

John Lennon
"Imagine"
memorial

Calvin the Cat

paper-airplane-type
note thing left by
tourist (and/or huge
John Lennon fan)

Then we got into a semi-big argument
in Strawberry Fields about where to go
next. It was loud enough that at one
point, this hippie with an acoustic
guitar stopped playing "Yesterday"
and went "Shhhhhh! This is a sacred
space!"

Which was RIDICULOUS. "Yesterday"
isn't even a John Lennon song. Everybody
knows Paul McCartney wrote it.

Eventually, we decided to go east and
hit Dylan's Candy Bar and Bloomingdale's.
But that wound up taking forever.

First, we had to go all the way back
across the park to Fifth Avenue. Then we
couldn't get a cab.

So we wound up having to basically run
the whole way, which made everybody sweaty
and mad.

And I think Jens was starting to get
a blister.

JENS

My shoes were very wrong for running.
Also my socks were not good, either.
(but very cute)

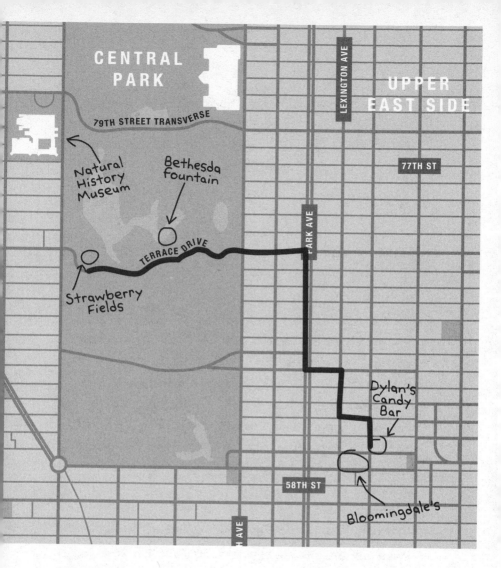

CLAUDIA

Because we were running the whole time, nobody stopped to check the hunt's ClickChat wall.

So it was a huge shock when we ran into Ling the Fembot coming out of Dylan's Candy Bar with this giant shopping bag that looked like it weighed twenty pounds.

PARVATI

I was like, "Ling? Hello? You got disqualified!"

CARMEN

Ling snorted and went, "You wish!"

Then she did that obnoxious hair-toss thing I swear is going to give her whiplash some day. At least, I hope it does.

Then her chauffeur or whatever held the door open while she got in the back of her car. And when she drove off, she yelled, "Good luck with the jelly beans!"

CLAUDIA

I remember thinking, "A) What does she mean about the jelly beans? And B) why is she still getting stuff when she's been disqualified?"

So we all took out our phones and checked the ClickChat wall.

CLICKCHAT POSTS ON "CULVERT PREP SCAVENGER HUNT" WALL

Athena's mom

goddessgurrl This is Athena Cohen's mother and the chaperone of Goddesses, Inc. Your decision to disqualify our team under paragraph 2 is without merit and must be reversed immediately.

Akash

CzarOfTheHunt Umm...sorry. But no.

Natasha (Wut Ups)

tasha_sez Is 500 pts for Deondra pic real

CzarOfTheHunt DEONDRA PIC IS A JOKE. Quit asking, people

goddessgurrl Paragraph 2 of rule sheet states "team members SHOULD remain together." It does NOT say "MUST remain together." Under this language, remaining together is clearly not obligatory, and you must reinstate us.

CzarOfTheHunt It IS obligatory. Teams have to stick together.

goddessgurrl That is not what your rule says.

CzarOfTheHunt Yes, it does.

goddessgurrl No, it doesn't. I am a Harvard-trained lawyer, and I can assure you my interpretation is correct. Reinstate us immediately.

Hunter (Killaz)

nightstaker wow this is cray

CzarOfTheHunt The rule is clear. Teams have to stick together.

goddessgurrl No. Your rule states only that they SHOULD remain together. Comparatively, para. 3 states "Each team MUST have an adult chaperone." This indicates a material distinction: "Must" is compulsory; "should" is desirable but NOT compulsory. Therefore, Goddesses, Inc., cannot be disqualified.

CzarOfTheHunt That is very nit-picky.

goddessgurrl Regardless, it is correct. Reinstate us now.

CzarOfTheHunt I can't. Mrs. Bevan disqualified you.

goddessgurrl I AM A HARVARD-TRAINED LAWYER. If you do not reinstate Goddesses, Inc., I will contest this decision to the fullest legal extent, with severe consequences for both Culvert Prep and the hunt's organizers, yourself included.

CzarOfTheHunt Are you saying you're going to sue me?

goddessgurrl Yes. And I will seek substantial damages.

nightstaker OHH SNAP **** JUST GOT REAL

CzarOfTheHunt This is Mrs. Bevan typing on Akash's account—Mrs. Cohen, is there a number where I can reach you?

goddessgurrl 917-5~~~~~~~

J_KOPP this is nuts! *[handwritten label: Josh (Gingivitis)]*

nightstaker ikr? pass the popcorn yall

daniR anyone know where to find Deondra *[handwritten label: Daniella R. (The Fierceness)]*

J_KOPP Deondra was a joke duh. Not real

daniR To bad I wantd to meet her

J_KOPP yah right good luck with that

CzarOfTheHunt NOTICE TO ALL TEAMS: REMAINING TOGETHER IS *NOT* STRICTLY REQUIRED UNDER THE RULES. HOWEVER, IT IS STRONGLY RECOMMENDED FOR SAFETY REASONS. PLEASE STICK TOGETHER AT ALL TIMES IF POSSIBLE.

CzarOfTheHunt Also: Goddesses, Inc. has been reinstated. Organizers sincerely apologize for any misunderstanding.

[handwritten note: NOTE: head exploded here]

CLAUDIA

That's when my head exploded.

And then it got worse. Because when we went down to the basement of Dylan's Candy Bar to get three buttered-popcorn flavor jelly beans (four points), we found this:

↙ EMPTY!!!

Suddenly, the fact that Ling was carrying a giant (and very heavy) bag when she walked out the door made perfect (and very evil) sense.

She'd bought EVERY SINGLE buttered-popcorn jelly bean.

So not only had Athena's "Harvard-trained lawyer" mom just raised the Fembots from the dead like zombies, but now they were sabotaging everybody else.

And I was just minutes away from a major fight with Mom in the middle of the Bloomingdale's furniture department.

CHAPTER 13
MY DAD MAKES A SERIOUSLY
BAD JUDGMENT CALL

good decision

bad decision

REESE

It turned out the favor Dad wanted in return for buying the Cronut was for us to go to his office with him so he could work.

He was like, "I just need to put out a fire. Ten minutes. And there's free snacks! What do you say?"

We basically went nuts on him. Because now that we had a 30-point Cronut, we figured we were winning—and there was NO WAY we were going to blow our lead by wasting a bunch of time at his office.

When Dad realized we wouldn't go for it, he said, "Let me see that list again."

He looked it over for a second. Then he went, "Okay, what if..." ←—*bad judgment starts here*

Then he stopped and chewed his lip for a second, like he was really stressed out.

Then he went, "I'm going to suggest something...but you guys have to promise me you'll NEVER TELL ANYONE—"

And James yelled, "STRANGER DANGER!"

So Xander had to put him in another headlock
to keep him quiet.

JAMES

I know a kidnapping attempt when I see one.

REESE

Basically, Dad offered to drop us off at
the Staten Island Ferry, then go to his office
while we rode the ferry and got the Statue of
Liberty pic—which was ten points—then meet
us back at the Wall Street bull statue. Which
was three points and right between the ferry
terminal and Dad's office.

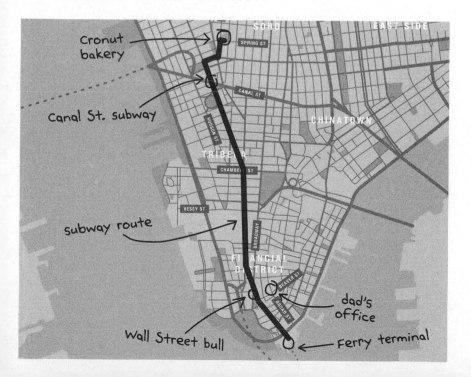

Cronut
bakery

Canal St. subway

subway route

Wall Street bull

dad's
office

Ferry terminal

We knew not having a chaperone could get
you disqualified. But we figured if it was just
for the ferry ride, we wouldn't get busted.

Plus, Dad gave us each twenty bucks to
stay quiet.

CLAUDIA

If you're reading this and thinking,
"This is starting to get ethically sketchy,
and Claudia's dad is showing incredibly bad
judgment," I definitely agree.

REESE

We couldn't find a minivan cab downtown,
so we had to take the subway at Canal
Street. When we got down to the platform,
the display said the next train to South
Ferry was in 4 minutes.

Which was, like, EXACTLY enough time for our Calvin the Cat to fall on the tracks and get splacked by a train. N.A.A.W.

I don't want to get into a whole big thing about whose fault that was. But it definitely wasn't mine, Dad's, or Wyatt's.

XANDER

My hands was clean, yo. Alls I did was stuff dem cat down the back of J-Mo's shirt. And then defend my space when he tried to stuff it down MY shirt.

If J-Mo hadn't come at me with that ish, I wouldn'a had to smack dem cat 'cross the platform.

JAMES

I have a theory: The cat had a death wish.

I don't know why. It's not like I can tell you what was going on in its head. Or what was left of its head, because it lost a lot of stuffing when that truck hit it.

But I think it's pretty clear the cat wanted to die.

Also: It did NOT have nine lives. It had maybe three. At the most.

REESE

When the train hit the cat, we totally freaked. Because without the cat, we couldn't take any pictures!

So we knew we had to get it back. But when something falls on the subway tracks, you ABSOLUTELY DEFINITELY can't go get it yourself. It's crazy dangerous, and if you try, you can get killed super-easily.

At least, that's what Dad said after he screamed at Xander for almost trying it. Like, louder than I've ever heard Dad scream in his life.

But it turns out a lot of subway stations have a station manager. And if you find that guy, he can call somebody and get them to hold all the trains coming down the line while another guy shows up with this weird-looking pair of big rubber tongs and uses them to get your Calvin off the tracks.

Or in this case, both parts of your Calvin. Because the subway wheels split it right down the middle.

subway tracks
(v. dangerous)

Calvin
(head)

Calvin
(not head)

subway
platform
(v. dirty)

We also found out if you get a station manager to stop all the trains because you dropped something super-important on the tracks, and he finds out the super-important thing was a stuffed animal, he'll get really, REALLY mad and swear at your dad. In both English and Spanish.

But you'll still get your stuffed animal parts back.

Long story short, twenty minutes later, we were outside the Staten Island Ferry.

Staten Island Ferry

Dad showed us which street the Wall Street bull statue was on, and he was like, "Text me when you're halfway back on the ferry and I'll meet you in front of the bull."

WYATT

And I was like, "Wait—how often do the ferries run?"

And your dad was like, "Every half hour."

Then we did the math, and we realized it was going to take at LEAST an hour just to get that one photo.

XANDER

I's all, "Too much time, yo! We gots to split up!"

And I could peep Big Daddy Tapper fixin'
to shut that down HARD—but then some dawg
from his office hit him on his cell.

REESE

Dad was like, "You HAVE to promise me
you'll all stick together." ~~N.A.A.W.~~
Which was cray, because we'd just found
out on ClickChat that sticking together
wasn't even a rule anymore.

But before we could argue with him, he
got a call from his boss. And he did the
"I'm-holding-up-a-finger-which-means-this-
is-super-important-and-don't-talk-to-me"
thing.

So we were like, "Umm...BYE!" And we
ran into the ferry terminal before Dad could
get off the phone.

I think we figured we'd just split up
for a little while. And it wouldn't be a big
deal, because we'd find a bunch more stuff
and get back in plenty of time to meet Dad.
So instead of waiting for him to get off
the phone and having a big argument, it was
better to just run off on him.

So that was our bad.

CHAPTER 13½
MY DAD WANTS YOU TO KNOW
HE IS NOT A HORRIBLE PERSON

CLAUDIA

I don't ordinarily interview Mom and Dad when I'm putting together an oral history like this one, because I believe their text messages speak for themselves.

But in this case, I am making an exception.

Mostly because Dad begged me to let him tell his side of the story. *also threatened me (with loss of laptop/ phone privileges)*

DAD (aka Eric Tapper, aka male parent of Claudia and Reese)

Hey, kiddo.

CLAUDIA

Hi, Dad.

DAD

First of all, I really appreciate the opportunity to—

CLAUDIA

Just the facts, Dad. Make it quick.

DAD

Okay. Will do.

So, umm...You know Daddy loves you and your brother very much, right? And your personal safety is incredibly important to him, and he'd never do anything to put either of you at risk except in extremely unusual circumstances. Right?

CLAUDIA

Oh, sure.

DAD

And you also know it's VERY expensive to live in New York City. Right? And it's even MORE expensive to go to a school like Culvert Prep. And both your dad and your mom have to work INCREDIBLY HARD to earn enough money to pay for all of it. You know that, right?

CLAUDIA

Where are you going with this, Dad?

DAD

Daddy has a very challenging job. At a very large law firm. Working directly under a man who...well, basically, he's evil.

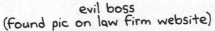

evil boss
(found pic on law firm website)

pitchfork
(NOT found
on law firm
website)

tail

So Daddy has an evil boss. And Daddy's
evil boss—

CLAUDIA

Can you stop talking about yourself in
the third person? It's weird.

DAD

You're right. I'm sorry. I don't know
why I was doing that.

CLAUDIA

I don't, either. It's very condescending.

condescending

condescending | ˌkän-də-ˈsen-ding | adjective |
acting in a manner that shows the speaker feels a sense
of superiority to the listener

DAD

> Nice job using "condescending" properly.

CLAUDIA

> Thank you. I read a lot.

DAD

> I know you do. You're a great kid.

CLAUDIA

> We're getting sidetracked here.

DAD

> Right. Where were we?

CLAUDIA

> Evil boss.

DAD

> Oh, yeah. So, I work for a man who doesn't

have a whole lot in the way of human compassion. Or any appreciation for work-life balance, or the demands of being a parent...

CLAUDIA

We get it. He's evil. What else?

DAD

Okay, so...on the morning of the scavenger hunt, there was a merger happening between two very large companies. And Daddy's law firm—sorry, MY law firm—was representing one of them. And there was some uncertainty about the tax implications of the merger.

And so Daddy's—sorry, MY—evil boss basically said, "If you don't come into the office and get this sorted out RIGHT THIS INSTANT, your job will no longer exist and you will have no money for food. Or private school tuition."

EVEN MORE crazy (Dad won't tell me how much)

So I didn't have a choice. I HAD to go into the office. Or lose my job.

↖ CRAZY expensive in NYC (grilled cheese at diner now $6.95)

CLAUDIA

I totally get that. And I, personally, would NOT want you to lose your job.

But why did you lie to Mom about the
whole thing?

DAD

>Okay, that...um...
>That was...uh, I, um...
>That was an error in judgment.
>Yeah. Big error. Definitely a mistake.

CLAUDIA

>Mom thinks so, too.

DAD

I know. We've talked about it. Kind of
a lot, actually.

very true
(Mom having hard time
letting go of this one)

CHAPTER 14
MOM AND I GET IN A HUGE FIGHT IN THE BLOOMINGDALE'S FURNITURE DEPARTMENT

CLAUDIA

Technically, my huge fight with Mom started while we were crossing Third Avenue to get from Dylan's Candy Bar to Bloomingdale's. Which is an awesome but crazy expensive department store—although, tbh, until I saw "photo of price tag for item over $100,000 (8 points)" on the list, I did not realize just how crazy it could get.

BLOOMINGDALE'S (aka Bloomie's)

The fight was about whether Team Melting Pot could split up. With the Fembots and their fleet of limos back in business, it seemed obvious there was no way we could beat them unless we went in at LEAST two different directions.

It got even more obvious when we ran into Kalisha Hendricks in women's perfume. She was leaving the elevators and moving fast.

CARMEN

Kalisha saw us all together and went, "You guys know it's okay to split up, right?"

The way she said it, you could tell she was thinking, "And if you DON'T split up, you are DOOMED."

Actually, she must have figured we were already doomed. Because Kalisha's super-competitive—so if she thought we were a threat, she probably wouldn't have given us the jelly beans.

KALISHA, Avada Kedavra team member ^ also very smart (and competitive) person

I had extras, because the buttered-popcorn jelly bean dispenser went psycho and dumped about twenty of them into my bag.

And when you told me how Ling had

bought them all, I was totally psyched to
share mine. Because that's just not right.

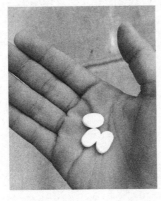

buttered popcorn jelly beans
(courtesy of Kalisha)

PARVATI

Can I just say, Kalisha was totally
cool and the nicest person ever? AND she
told us where to find the Bloomie's item.

CLAUDIA

Right before she ran off, Kalisha
turned back to us and said, "FYI, the thing
you're looking for in here? Fifth floor."

But like Carmen said, Kalisha's super-
competitive. So I was a little skeptical.

PARVATI

"A little skeptical?" Excuse me? You
yelled, "IT'S A TRAP! SHE'S HEAD-FAKING US!"

CLAUDIA

I did NOT yell. I was very calmly pointing out a logical possibility.

CARMEN

I'm sorry, but you were NOT calm. You wouldn't even get on the elevator. I was all, "Oh, sure, Claudia—and the jelly beans are PROBABLY POISONED." (Sarcasm)

PARVATI

Kalisha's SO boss. We would've kicked SO much butt if she was on our team.

CLAUDIA

Do NOT start with that. And BTW, that crack about Kalisha's shoes was totally uncalled for. And seriously mean to Jens.

PARVATI

All I did was point out that Kalisha was wearing running shoes. Which were NOT giving her blisters. And Jens didn't even get that I was flaming him. Because he can't speak English.

CLAUDIA

I am not even going there.

So we went up to the fifth floor and started checking the tags on couches and dresser sets. Which were mostly in the $10,000 range—so, ridiculously expensive, but not nearly ridiculous enough.

5 fifth level fashions for her
fashions for the home

dresses
swim
furniture
mattresses
rugs
corporate services

Bloomie's 5th floor
(no idea what
"corporate
services" are)

And that's when my fight with Mom really got going. Because even though it was obvious we ABSOLUTELY HAD TO SPLIT UP, Mom kept insisting she didn't have permission from Carmen, Parvati, and Jens's parents to let them "wander around the city alone."

Which was very annoying, because A) they wouldn't be "wandering," they'd be RUNNING (depending on their shoes); and B) nobody would even be alone, because we could only split into as many teams as we had Calvins. And we could only get one more Calvin.

CARMEN

I still had mine from kindergarten.

I was going to throw it away last year,
but my mom was like, "It's a memento!"

I thought she was being ridic, but it
definitely came in handy.

CLAUDIA

Mostly, the fight was just me vs.
Mom, because even though Parvati and
Carmen were on my side, you can't fight
with somebody else's mom. It's sort of an
unwritten rule.

And Jens just kind of hung back and
pretended he wasn't with us, because he is
not comfortable around conflict.

Occasionally, Mom would pause the fight
to text Dad, asking for his opinion. Which,
considering that he'd just left Reese's
team wandering around the city alone, was
completely insane.

But Mom didn't know that.

MOM AND DAD (text messages)

Did you see ClickChat wall?

No

Apparently teams can split up. Claudia wants to. I think terrible idea bc not safe for kids to be wandering alone in city w no parent

Probably not so bad

You're not letting your team split up, are you?

No they're together

I should def tell Claudia no, right?

your call

But whole point of chaperoning is making sure kids are safe. Right?

guess so

Claudia furious. V stressful. Tell me it's ok to stand my ground and make kids stick together even if it hurts team

Seriously, what should I do? Feel like bad mother either way

Eric?

in mtg

How can you be in a meeting?

sorry in hurry

Calling you now

can't talk

Y not??

on subway

no reception

Then how can you send texts?

g2g

CLAUDIA

It took forever, but I finally came up with a plan that Mom couldn't argue with: she'd take Parvati and Carmen with her, and Jens and I would go off by ourselves.

This made sense, because A) Mom would still be chaperoning Parvati and Carmen; B) Mom had to admit I was a responsible enough person to go off by myself as long as I wasn't alone; and C) Jens and I convinced her that his parents are very laid-back and would be totally fine with it.

In fact, Jens's parents are so laid-back that he wasn't even sure if they knew he was at a scavenger hunt.

JENS

Dutch parents are not so...how do you say it...?

CLAUDIA

Uptight?

JENS

Yes. The Dutch are more downloose.

*not a word
(but VERY cute)*

CLAUDIA

Right when Mom finally downloosed, Carmen found the rugs.

rug department

CARMEN

OMG I CANNOT BELIEVE HOW MUCH THOSE RUGS COST!

CLAUDIA

The rug department was right next to furniture, and the second we started checking tags on the handwoven Persians, it was obvious we'd hit the jackpot.

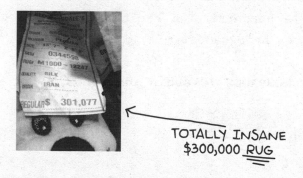

TOTALLY INSANE
$300,000 RUG

PARVATI

All I could think was, "What if you had a dog...and you bought that rug...and the dog peed on it?"

I mean, seriously. Can you imagine? Do rich people not have dogs or something?

CARMEN

I think there might be a secret department in the basement of Bloomingdale's where you can buy dogs that don't pee or poop. To go with your $300,000 rug.

The dogs are, like, $400,000.

CLAUDIA

Finding the rug (eight points!) put everybody in a good mood. Then Mom went with Parvati and Carmen to get more items on the East Side, while Jens and I headed for Times Square and the West Side.

Although first I had to find Jens, because he'd temporarily disappeared.

TEXT MESSAGES (Claudia and Jens)

WHERE R U???????

Shoe department. Do you like?
Better for running

OMG GET BACK TO FURNITURE
RIGHT NOW

BUT FIRST BUY THE SHOES

CHAPTER 15
MY BROTHER'S TEAM
GETS IN SERIOUS TROUBLE

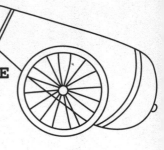

CLAUDIA

While I am a very responsible person who can definitely be left alone in the middle of Manhattan for longer than ten minutes without causing a major disaster, my brother is not.

And neither are his idiot friends.

REESE

There were a TON of people waiting to get on the Staten Island Ferry. Which was kind of surprising, because minor-league baseball season was over. And if you're not going to see a Staten Island Yankees game, I don't know why you'd go to Staten Island.

Staten Island
Ferry crowd

CLAUDIA

Maybe because, I don't know, you live there? Like HALF A MILLION people do?

Manhattan →

New Jersey

FINANCIAL DISTRICT

CHAMBERS ST

VESEY ST

Ellis Island

ferry route →

Governors Island ↓

Statue of Liberty ↓

Brooklyn

Staten Island
(HALF A MILLION PEOPLE!!)

REESE

Oh. Right. That makes sense. Wow, it must be a pretty big island.

Anyway, Xander told Wyatt to get on the ferry and take a pic of Calvin with the Statue of Liberty in the background.

WYATT

I said, "Why do I have to do it?"

XANDER

I was all, "I ain't doin' it."

REESE

I was like, "I get seasick. For reals." Which is totally true. I'm a barfer.

Unfortunately true (also happens in back seat of cars) (#HardToLiveWith)

JAMES

There's a warrant for my arrest in Staten Island. I can't set foot there.

REESE

I seriously doubt that's true. But whatever.

WYATT

So I said, "I don't want to go to Staten Island alone!"

REESE

And I went, "Somebody's gotta do it. Why don't we take a vote?"

So we did.

The results were three votes for Wyatt and one vote for "anybody but Wyatt."

WYATT

That was totally unfair of you guys.

REESE

Then Wyatt tried to get out of going. He was like, "We can't split up—we've only got one Calvin the Cat!"

JAMES

I said, "Actually, we have two. You want the head or the legs?"

WYATT

I took the legs. 'Cause the head had fallen in some kind of sewer water on the subway tracks, so it smelled really nasty.

SO disgusting—can't believe nobody got incurable disease

REESE

We left Wyatt in the ferry line, and we

walked out of the terminal thinking, "We are going to crush this!"

But then we realized we didn't have a list of the scavenger hunt items. Dad had our only copy, and nobody'd remembered to take it before we ran off.

JAMES

For a person with a photographic memory, this was not a problem.

But none of us had a photographic memory.

So it was a problem.

REESE

We spent a couple of minutes going, "What was that thing in Times Square...?" And "Something, something Chinatown...?"

All we could remember for sure were the FAO Schwarz piano and the Coney Island Cyclone, which is this awesome roller coaster way out on the edge of Brooklyn.

Then Xander was like, "Bull pic, yo!"

So we walked over to the Wall Street bull statue and got that for three points.

Reese says Xander made them shoot rear view, which is TOTALLY IMMATURE

Then we decided to go to Coney Island.

XANDER

I was all, "Cyclone, yo! Mad points for that bad boy!" So I peeped Coney Island on Google Maps, and we needed to mack the 4 train, then hook up a transfer.

So we wuz gonna hit the subway. But then we peeped the bar showing Man U-Liverpool.

REESE

Xander's second-favorite soccer team is Manchester United. They were playing Liverpool that day, and there was this big sign on the sidewalk outside this bar that said "WATCH MAN UNITED VS. LIVERPOOL ON THE BIG SCREEN!"

Right when we walked past the bar, we heard all this cheering, like somebody'd just scored.

And Xander was all, "Let's check the score, yo!"

And I was like, "We don't have time for this!" But Xander had already gone inside. So James and I followed him.

Hooligans was here (closed a week after hunt & became a Duane Reade) (eventually, EVERY place in NYC closes & becomes a Duane Reade)

CLAUDIA

You do know it's illegal for a 12-year-old to walk into a bar without a parent, right?

REESE

Well, I do NOW. I didn't know then.

I also didn't realize the bar was
called Hooligans. Which is, like, NOT a
great name for a bar that shows English
soccer matches.

Also, it's a VERY bad idea to
walk into a bar like that with James
Mantolini.

*For more info,
google "English
soccer hooligans."
It is CRAZY*

JAMES

I'm not really into sports. So to me,
it just looked like a bunch of loud, sweaty
guys yelling at a TV.

And I thought, y'know...join the fun.

REESE

So we get in there, and it was definitely
a Liverpool bar, because it was totally
packed with their fans. It was, like, this
army of giant bald guys in red jerseys.

And Xander had totally disappeared.

XANDER

I was hittin' the little boys' room.
X-Man needed to tinkle.

REESE

Liverpool had just scored, so the whole bar was doing this victory chant. They had super-thick accents, so it was hard to understand what the chant was. But it was definitely dirty. And it was REALLY mean to Man U's fans. And their players. And the players' moms.

And right when the chant finished, there was this moment of quiet where nobody was yelling anything.

And that's when James screamed, "LIVERPOOL SUCKS!"

↖ really, really, REALLY not smart to do this in bar full of giant Liverpool fans

JAMES

I was just trying to get in the spirit of it. Everybody else was yelling stuff. So I thought they'd appreciate hearing a wider variety of opinions about their little soccer team.

But they definitely did not appreciate that. So they tried to kill us.

REESE

Fortunately, we were right by the front door. If we'd been, like, ten feet farther away from it, I think we'd literally be dead right now.

The next couple of minutes are kind of hard to remember. I know we were running, and I was really, really scared. And a bunch of the Liverpool fans were chasing us. I'm not sure how many.

XANDER

Alls I know is, when I came out of the can, half the bar was gone.

Which was beast, 'cause then there were free seats! So I copped one and started to peep the game.

And I ordered some wings. 'Cause X-Man was hungry.

REESE

I have definitely never been that scared in my whole life. I was running flat out, so I couldn't look back. But we could hear the Liverpool guys screaming at us. They were going, "WE'RE GOING TO KILL YOU!" Only with really thick accents. And a lot of swear words.

And the streets in that part of town are crazy narrow and short, so we kept, like, skurtling around corners looking for a place to hide. *N.A.A.W.*

S.N.A.A.W. (STILL Not An Actual Word) And we skurtled around this one corner, and there was a delivery truck sitting there with its back door wide open. And it was totally dark inside it.

delivery truck (not actual truck) (but Reese says it looked just like this one)

And all of a sudden, James jumped into the back of the truck and disappeared.

So I followed him.

JAMES

Now that I think about it, Reese never once thanked me for saving his life by jumping in the back of that truck. He was actually kind of ungrateful.

REESE

You were the whole reason we were running for our lives!

JAMES

But I also SAVED our lives. So it balances out.

REESE

Whatever.

So James and I got all crouched down behind the boxes. And we heard the, like, "RAAAAH!" of all the soccer guys running by.

Then it got quiet, and we were about to stand up and get out of there. But then we heard somebody coming, so we ducked down again. And a second later, there was this crazy-loud shuddery rumble.

Which must have been the roller door of the truck coming down. Because all of a sudden, it was pitch black, and we couldn't see a thing.

Then a second later, we heard the front door open and close real fast. Then the engine started.

And that's how we got trapped in the back of a truck headed for New Jersey.

CHAPTER 16
SABOTAGE IN TIMES SQUARE

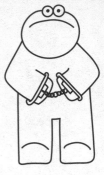

CLAUDIA

Even though Jens had lived in New York City for over three months, he'd never been on the subway before, because his mom is scared of it. So it was very exciting for him to take the 6 to Grand Central and then transfer to the shuttle to Times Square.

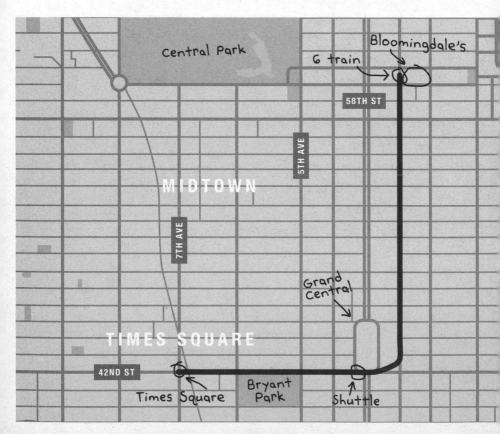

JENS

I was surprised. I thought there would be a bad smell, but it was okay.

CLAUDIA

It only smells really bad in the summer.

Times Square subway station
   (smell not pictured)

We were headed to Times Square for two things: a Playbill from a Broadway musical (5 points) and a picture of a guy in a Flubby suit holding Calvin the Cat (8 points).

Getting the Playbill was easy. All we had to do was go to a theater and beg.

VERY funny play
(convinced Mom to take me
2 weeks after scavenger hunt)
(ALSO: Dad says for legal
reasons, I HAVE to say
"Playbill did NOT endorse
this scavenger hunt")

But pointwise, the really important thing was the Flubby picture. In case you were never a kid and/or grew up without a television, Flubby is a character on the show *Aardvark Avenue.* He's basically a rock star to every three-year-old in the world.

JENS

In the Netherlands, he is not Flubby. He's *Fluuber.*

SO cute

CLAUDIA

On most days, there are half a dozen people in Flubby suits wandering around Times Square, charging tourists money to take pictures with them.

Flubby

tourist

tourist's money

It's a little weird, but then so are a
lot of things in Times Square.

It didn't take us long to find a Flubby,
and he seemed totally happy to let me take
his picture...until I pulled our Calvin out
of my bag.

When he saw the Calvin, he started
shaking his big Flubby head side to side,
like he was saying, "Nooooo."

I figured it was because I hadn't tipped
him yet, so I pulled out a few dollars and
offered them to him. When I did, he started
waving his arms, like, "No, no, no!"

I said, "Why not?"

Then he turned his back on me and ran away.

Flubby
(running away)

Considering how much *Aardvark Avenue* I watched when I was little, having a Flubby run away from me like that was actually kind of upsetting.

But it was about to get much more upsetting.

JENS

It was very strange at first. All the *Fluubers*, when they saw the Calvin, folded their arms and would not hold him.

CLAUDIA

It was like they were vampire Flubbies,

and our Calvin was made of garlic. Every
time we walked up to a Flubby, he'd be all,
"Oh, hi!" friendly—but as soon as I pulled
out the Calvin, he'd freak out and refuse to
hold it.

When it happened with the fifth Flubby
in a row, I got very frustrated. So I
yelled, "Why won't you hold it? It's just a
cat!" at him.

And this muffled, echo-y voice from
inside the Flubby head said, "I promised the
girl no one else!" in a Spanish accent.

"What girl?" I said.

"The rich girl," said Spanish Flubby.

Right away, I knew what had
happened: Fembot sabotage.

"Did a girl pay you not to take any
pictures with these cats?" I asked him.

Spanish Flubby nodded his giant head.

"What did she look like?"

"Long hair. Black car. Nice clothes."
Athena Cohen.

Actually, it could have been Meredith.
Or Ling. Or Clarissa. Depending on how much
she'd paid him and how nice the clothes were.

"How much did she pay you?"

"Fifty dollar."

other Flubbies
who rejected us:
—angry Flubby
—lazy Flubby
(wore Crocs)
—fur-falling-
out Flubby
—red Flubby
(might actually
have been
Elmo)

Definitely Athena. Only she was rich and evil enough to pay off every Flubby in Times Square.

"Can't you just please take this one picture?" I begged him. "She'll never know!"

"No," said Spanish Flubby. "I make a promise."

"Please?"

"No. Sorry. Flubby is role model for the children. Flubby has to keep promises."

actually very admirable of him (but annoying)

JENS

When you kept asking him and the *Fluuber* kept saying no, you looked so sad. I just wanted to make you cheer up.

CLAUDIA

Jens gave me a hug and said, "Don't worry. It's just a game. Let's go eat lunch."

Which actually made me REALLY mad. Because I felt like if we couldn't even get an 8-point Flubby picture, we'd definitely lose to the Fembots. And I didn't want Jens to be okay with that—I wanted him to get mad and kick butt with me.

But before I could tell him that, I

heard another inside-a-Flubby-head voice
yell, "Hey! Kid!"

I turned around, and one of the other
Flubbies was standing there. I'm not sure if
it was one of the Flubbies who'd turned us
down or a totally new Flubby. It's very hard
to tell them apart. may have been "angry Flubby"
(see above)

He said, "You wanna picture wit' da
cat?"

This Flubby had that kind of
"Fuhgeddaboudit!" New York accent that cab
drivers have in bad movies. (Which, BTW, is
RIDICULOUS, because most NYC cab drivers are
from foreign countries and don't sound like
that at all.)

I said, "Yes! Will you do it?"

Fuhgeddaboudit Flubby said, "Fifty
bucks."

Which was crazy, because I am not
Athena Cohen. Plus it was impossible,
because I only had twenty-three dollars
on me. So I was about to say, "How about
twenty?"

But then Spanish Flubby waved his big
furry finger at Fuhgeddaboudit Flubby and
yelled, "You cannot do this! You promise the
girl! You take her money!"

Fuhgeddaboudit Flubby told Spanish
Flubby to get lost. Only he used language
you seriously do NOT want to hear coming
from a Flubby. *if any 3-year-olds heard him, they are probably scarred for life*
Spanish Flubby said something like,
"Shame to you! Shame! You wear Flubby
costume! You must have honor!"

Then Fuhgeddaboudit Flubby punched
Spanish Flubby in the head.

I don't think it hurt, because it wasn't his real head. It was his giant fake head.

But then they started kicking each other, and THAT looked like it hurt.

Then they REALLY went at it. I freaked out and started screaming. I'm not sure if that was the right thing to do, but it's not like I'd ever spent any time thinking about how I'd react if I saw two Flubbies beating each other up in Times Square.

While I was screaming, Jens took pictures.

JENS

At first, I thought, "This is very bad! We have to get away!"

But then I thought, "Two *Fluubers* fighting—probably I never see this in my life again. I should take pictures."

CLAUDIA

Fortunately, it was Times Square, so there were two cops very close by. And when I screamed, they ran over and stopped the fight.

Then they asked us who started it. We told them Fuhgeddaboudit Flubby threw the first punch, so they put him in handcuffs.

no photo of Flubby in handcuffs
(b/c cop told Jens not cool to take one)

Then we got out of there in a hurry, because I knew if they made us go to the police station to make a statement, we'd never get back to the hunt.

For the record, though, I'd like to point out that the Flubby-on-Flubby violence never would have happened if Athena Cohen hadn't paid all the Flubbies off in the first place.

I'd also like to point out that we didn't get the 8-point Flubby photo. And without it, Team Melting Pot was basically doomed.

Unless we could somehow come up with a brilliant, game-changing plan.

But that's a story for another chapter.

(specifically, Chapter 18)

CHAPTER 17
MY BROTHER IS TRAPPED
IN A DELIVERY TRUCK
HEADED FOR THE
HOLLAND TUNNEL

CLAUDIA

By this point, Dad's work crisis was over. But his scavenger hunt crisis was just getting started.

REESE

I was seriously freaking out in the back of that truck. 'Cause it was really loud and bouncy, and there was, like, no light at all except from our phones.

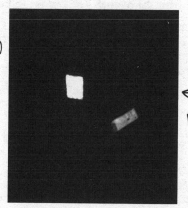

view from
back of truck
(artist's re-creation)
(took this inside
our bathroom)

light from phones

James and I were going, "HELLO? Mister Truck Driver? Please help us!" But he couldn't hear us. I think he had the radio on really loud or something.

James was all, "We are DEFINITELY going to die back here."

And I was like, "How?"

And James was like, "Probably starvation."

When he said that, I kind of panicked.

That's why I ate the Cronut.

CLAUDIA

I still can't believe you ate the Cronut. IT WAS THIRTY POINTS!

REESE

You don't know what it's like getting stuck in the back of a truck! It's really stressful!

I mean, I know we'd only been in there a couple of minutes. But I seriously didn't think I was ever going to eat again. And I didn't have a lot of breakfast that morning.

JAMES

I warned Reese not to eat the Cronut.

But once he started, I made him give
me half.

REESE

Right after we ate the Cronut—which
I'm pretty sure was real after all, because
it was mad delicious—I texted Dad.

**REESE AND DAD (Text messages copied from
Reese's phone)**

HELP DAD IM TRAPPED IN TRUCK

REESE

He must have still been in a meeting or
something, because he didn't text me back
right away. So I texted Mom.

**REESE AND MOM (Text messages copied from
Mom's phone)**

HELP MOM IM TRAPPED IN TRUCK

Is this a joke?

NO ITS SERIUS

REESE

Mom called me right away, and I told her everything that had happened.

And she was like, "Start screaming. Both of you. Top of your lungs."

So James and I started screaming.

And it worked! 'Cause right after that, the truck stopped. And we heard the driver get out, and we were like, "WE'RE BACK HERE!"

Then he rolled up the back door and let us out.

He was pretty mad.

JAMES

The truck driver seemed very unstable to me. Even more unstable than the soccer fans, to be honest.

truck driver
(artist's re-creation)
(based on eyewitness testimony)

REESE

He was going, "I'M GONNA HAVE YOUSE GUYS ARRESTED FOR TRESPASSIN'! DA COPS ARE GONNA PUT YOU IN JUVIE!"

Then James chucked the smelly Calvin head way up in the air.

Which he must have done to create a distraction—because while me and the truck driver were watching it come down, James took off running.

Like, he literally ran screaming down the street. Like, "AAAAAAAAAHH!"

JAMES

If you'd seen the truck driver, he was clearly not built for running long distances. So it seemed like a smart strategy.

REESE

Having James run off like that really crossed up the truck driver. He didn't know how to handle it. I could tell he was trying to think it through, like, "Should I chase that kid? Because then what if the other one gets away? And if I DON'T catch the first one, then NOBODY goes to juvie..."

Then he just gave up. He went, "Ahhh, nuts!" and drove away.

That's when I checked my phone and realized Dad had been texting me.

REESE AND DAD (Text messages copied from Reese's phone)

HELP DAD IM TRAPPED IN TRUCK

Where?

Reese? Are you joking?

Where are you?

Done with work—heading to bull statue—are you really trapped in a truck?

REESE PLEASE ANSWER

Its all good. Out of truck now

Where are you?

No idea. Maybe New Jersey?

he was NOT in New Jersey (but truck prob headed there b/c close to Holland Tunnel)

Are the others with you?

No Im alone

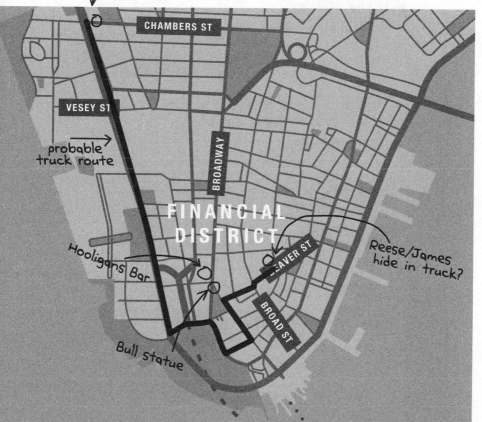

REESE

Dad and I talked on the phone, and when he figured out where I was, he told me to walk up Chambers Street to Broadway, then turn right and head downtown to meet him back at the bull statue.

Then he hung up real fast so he could try to track down the others.

WYATT AND DAD (Text messages copied from Wyatt's phone)

Wyatt, it's Reese's dad—where are you?

Staten Island. Took this pic

Statue of Liberty

Might be better to get shot with head

Other guys took head. Where r they

Where r others

Mr tapper?

g2g

meet at bull

XANDER AND DAD (Text messages copied from Xander's phone)

Xander, it's Reese's dad— where are you?

In a bar

Not a real bar, right?

No its real

Please leave immediately and meet at bull statue

Cant

Xander, you have to leave there now.
Meet at bull

But I ordered wingz

Xander can't spell a 5-letter word.
This is sad

Xander, IT IS ILLEGAL for you to be in a bar alone

wingz just got here

Xander, seriously, leave there now

Xander?

Have you left bar yet?

Cant txt sticky fingrs

JAMES AND DAD (Text messages copied from James's phone)

James, it's Reese's dad—where are you?

You have the wrong number

I am sorry.

James, are you sure this isn't you?

No one named James is at this number

This is the number listed in Culvert Prep online directory for James Mantolini

IF THIS HARASSMENT CONTINUES I WILL CALL THE POLICE

James, please stop joking. Where are you? As chaperone, it's my job to know where you are and that you are safe

YOUR BEHAVIOR IS ILLEGAL

THIS IS A FELONY

I HAVE FORWARDED YOUR NUMBER TO THE NYPD FOR INVESTIGATION

If this is not James, please accept my sincere apologies

REESE

That was totally James.

JAMES

Maybe it was, and maybe it wasn't.

CLAUDIA

It was. James let me copy the texts from his phone.

REESE

I seriously do not understand anything James Mantolini does.

So I walked up Chambers Street to Broadway like Dad had told me to. And while I was walking, I realized I forgot to tell Dad I'd talked to Mom. Which I think made things a lot worse for him.

MOM AND DAD (Text messages copied from Mom's phone)

Yep. Doing great

Kids are all fine?

Why do you ask?

Just curious. So, nothing to report?

A little hectic. But fine

Great!

Yes! Fun

So when my only son texts me "TRAPPED IN TRUCK AND AFRAID FOR MY LIFE" I should just text back "LOL"?

Calling you now

Honey?

Please answer phone

I can explain

Searching for best way to express my anger.

mushroom clouds from nuclear bombs (or just trees?) (but prob nukes)
Here we go:
I am so so sorry
Not as sorry as you will be

CHAPTER 18
JENS AND I COME UP
WITH A BRILLIANT,
GAME-CHANGING PLAN

CLAUDIA

After we got Fembotted in Times
Square, Jens and I headed downtown on the
1 train to get a bottle cap from the 5-cent
Coke machine at Tekserve (whatever that
was).

I was pretty upset about our whole
situation. It was 12:42pm, which meant the
hunt was almost half over, and there were
so many things on the list we hadn't gotten—
especially things that were ridiculously
far apart, like Yankee Stadium and Coney
Island—that it seemed like there was no way
we could win.

And with their four cars driving in
four different directions—and their insane
sabotaging of everybody—the Fembots were
probably crushing it.

Meanwhile, all Jens could think about
was having lunch.

JENS

    I was very interested to try this
Katz's Deli.

CLAUDIA

I told Jens that was ridiculous, and that he could drink the whole Coke from the 5-cent Coke machine (3 points), and MAYBE if we found a 99-cent pizza place (4 points), there'd be enough time to get a slice, but we were absolutely NOT going to take the time to sit down and eat, especially somewhere like Katz's Deli (5 points), which on a Saturday afternoon would be insanely crowded with tourists.

And also non-tourists, because the sandwiches at Katz's really are delicious.

Katz's Deli: try the pastrami (AMAZING)

But I didn't tell Jens that, because it just would have made him want to go there even more.

JENS

You were very stressed. So I said, "Why don't we be relaxed? Just have fun and not worry about winning?"

And that made you angry. You said, "This is not about fun! This is about justice!"

CLAUDIA

I really believed that. It wasn't just that we were going to lose. It was losing to the FEMBOTS, who were cheating up a storm.

And I wasn't just a player—I was the person who created the entire scavenger hunt! And if it turned out the only way you could win was by being completely evil and sabotaging everybody, it'd mean I had personally created a monster.

So no matter how much money we raised for the Manhattan Food Bank, the whole lesson of the hunt would be that the only way to get ahead in life is to be evil. (also rich)

Which would be a terrible, terrible thing, not just for this particular hunt, but for future generations.

So the stakes were a WHOLE lot higher than just "Let's have fun and go eat a corned beef on rye with some giant pickles."

even though that would be delicious (esp. at Katz's)

And when I explained all this to him, Jens totally changed his attitude.

JENS

I started to think, "How can we change the game so we win?"

So I look again at the list. And it is clear.

If we have a picture with Deondra, we get 500 points. And nobody can beat us.

CLAUDIA

At first, I was like, "Jens, Deondra kissing the Calvin was a JOKE. Haven't you heard that song?"

Because at the time of the hunt, that Deondra song "Cat's Kiss" was HUGE. So I figured that was why Akash had put it on the list.

TOP 10 SONGS FOR WEEK ENDING 10/25/14

1 CAT'S KISS, by Deondra

2 YOU CAN DO IT, Miranda Fleet

3 HIBBITY BIG, Fiddy K

AKASH

OF COURSE that's why I put it on the list!
DOES NO ONE IN THIS SCHOOL HAVE A SENSE
OF HUMOR?

JENS

I said, "So, okay. It's a joke. But still
it's on the list. So if we have a picture and
Deondra kisses the cat, we get 500 points."

CLAUDIA

I have no idea why I hadn't thought of that
myself. But I was so psyched Jens did that I
could've kissed him right there on the subway.

I'm not saying I actually DID kiss him.
Whether I did or not is nobody's business, so
I will neither confirm or deny it. *also he is NOT TECHNICALLY my boyfriend*

Either way, though, I was
thrilled. And also relieved—because
tbh, up until then Jens hadn't really been
pulling his weight.

As soon as we got out of the subway, I
called Parvati to tell her we needed to
devote all our resources to finding Deondra.

PARVATI

When you called, Carmen and I were waiting

in line with your mom to get the video of the
FAO Schwarz piano. And as soon as you mentioned
finding Deondra, I was like, "OMG, that is
BRILLIANT. And I can't believe I didn't think of
it first. Also, I'm totally the person to find
her, because I've been obsessed with Deondra
since fourth grade and I know every single
website that might help us track her down."

So right away, I got off the phone and
started searching.

CLAUDIA

Meanwhile, Jens and I went to Tekserve,
which turned out to be this really cool
computer store.

TEKSERVE
(worth a visit)
(and just 1 block from
Doughnut Plant!)
(also worth a visit)
(if you like doughnuts)

There was an old-fashioned Coke machine in the middle of the floor, and when we first got there, a guy in a Tekserve T-shirt had the door to the machine open.

That got me very worried. But when I said, "Hi! Is there any Coke left?" he replied, "Yeah, I'm just refilling it."

And then he said, "Some girl came in and emptied the whole machine. It was totally bizarre—she bought all the Cokes, dumped them out in the water fountain, and took the bottle caps with her. So after she left, I had to drag two more cases up from storage."

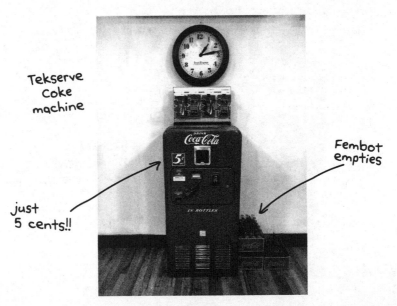

Tekserve Coke machine

Fembot empties

just 5 cents!!

bottle cap from 5-cent Coke

Knowing that a Fembot sabotage attempt
had been foiled made me think our luck was
turning—and when Parvati called me with her
Deondra update, I got even more hopeful.

PARVATI

Okay, so first I checked Deondra Online
to make sure she wasn't on tour, or filming
a movie, or, like, recording an album in
France. And she wasn't. So, all good.

Then I went to Fiddy K's website to
make sure HE wasn't on tour, because,
obvs, they're married and, like, totally
supportive of each other's careers. So if
he WAS touring, she'd probably be out there
with him.

And Fiddy K wasn't on tour, either. So,
still all good.

Then I went to OMG Celebrities In The

Wild! to see if Deondra had been spotted anywhere recently. And the last photo they had of her was, like, at a Starbucks in Miami. But that was two weeks ago, so I was like, STILL all good.

Then I checked Red Carpet 24/7—and THAT'S where I found out she and Fiddy K had just gone to a charity ball for autism at the Waldorf the night before.

And I was like, "OMG, this is PERFECT. Because they probably stayed out late, and then slept in, and I know from reading *I Am Deondra* that her favorite thing to do on the weekends is to walk her dog and/or go out to a totally low-key brunch with her husband and maybe a few close friends."

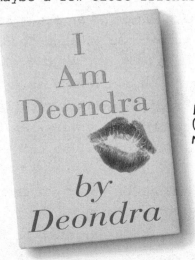

Deondra's autobiography (tbh, not as good as Miranda Fleet's *Fleeting*)

So I was like, "Claudia, you HAVE to get
over to Deondra's apartment building STAT
and wait for her to either come out and walk
her dog or go for brunch."

CLAUDIA

I was seriously impressed with Parvati's
detective work. My only question was, "Where
on earth is Deondra's apartment building?"

PARVATI

And I was like, "Duh! 511 Leonard Street
in TriBeCa! Everybody knows that!"
I totes would've gone myself, but we'd
been waiting to use that floor piano for, like,
twenty minutes. And I did NOT want to give
up our place in line. Especially since Colin
Hartley from Gingivitis was right behind us.

CLAUDIA

Jens and I googled the address, and two
minutes later, we were back on the 1 train
heading downtown to TriBeCa.
Incidentally, in the same way that "SoHo"
is short for "SOuth of HOuston," "TriBeCa" is
short for "TRIangle BElow CAnal Street."
Although for us, right then it was more

like, "**TRy**Ing to **BE**at the **CA**tty Fembots."

And for my dad, who happened to be very close by at that exact same moment, it was, "**TerRI**bly **BE**wildered 'Cause I Can't Find James Mantolini."

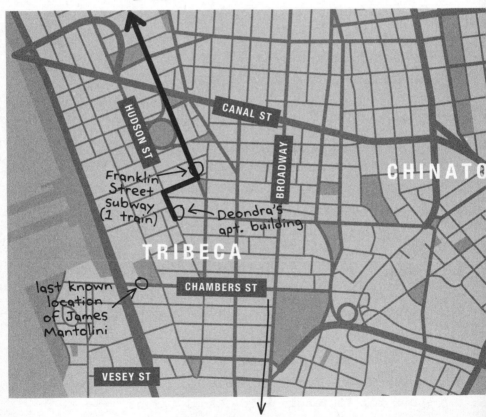

1 train

CANAL ST

HUDSON ST

BROADWAY

CHINATO

Franklin Street subway (1 train)

Deondra's apt. building

TRIBECA

last known location of James Mantolini

CHAMBERS ST

VESEY ST

Dad's office/bull statue/ Reese & idiot friends

CHAPTER 19
MY BROTHER'S TEAM
HITS A NEW LOW

REESE

When I got back to the bull statue,
Dad and Wyatt were already there. Dad was
majorly stressed about losing half our team,
and the first thing he did was take us back
to Hooligans to get Xander. I hid around the
corner with Wyatt so none of the Liverpool
fans would try to kill me again while Dad
dragged Xander outside.

XANDER

Yo, strong ups to Big Daddy Tapper for
frontin' the bill on dem wingz.

REESE

After that, we were like, "What's next
on the list?"

And Dad was like, "Finding James
Mantolini! What's his cell?"

And we were like, "Didn't he give it to
you when we started?"

And he was like, "Yeah, but it was fake. What's the real number?"

And we were like, "No idea."

Because none of us had ever called James for anything. But I had his email, 'cause he was on the cc list for kids who were supposed to be getting extra help in Ms. Santiago's math class during lunch.

So I emailed James, but I figured there was no way he'd get back to me.

REESE (email to James)

phone number crossed out b/c privacy

JAMES WHERE R U???????

From: skronkmonster@gmail.com
To: i_m_batman_4realz@yahoo.com
Date: 10/25/14 12:54:33 PM EDT
Subject: JAMES WHERE R U???????

MY DAD IS SUPER WORRIED PLZ CHECK IN W HIM

REESE

Then we were like, "Dad, don't worry, he's fine."

And Dad was like, "I'm the chaperone—I HAVE to make sure everybody's safe."

Which, seeing as how he'd left us alone in the first place, was, um...what's that word? When somebody says something, and it's like the opposite of what you'd expect?

CLAUDIA

Ironic?

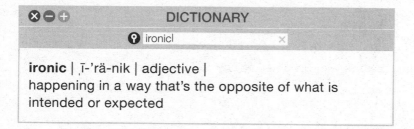

ironic | ī-'rä-nik | adjective |
happening in a way that's the opposite of what is intended or expected

REESE

That's it. Yeah. And it seemed totally cray to even try to look for James. 'Cause not only is New York City mega-huge, but we were in the middle of the scavenger hunt.

So we were all, "Why don't we just split up again?"

And Dad was like, "We are NOT splitting up! Over my dead body!" Which, again, was totally...oh, geez, I forgot that word already.

CLAUDIA

Ironic.

REESE

Right. Sorry.

And Wyatt and Xander were all, "We can't just quit the hunt! We're winning! We got the Cronut!"

So I had to tell them I ate the Cronut.

WYATT

I was seriously spun out over that. You stuck me on the ferry all alone—and then while I was gone, you ATE THE CRONUT?!

REESE

I am so skronking sorry, dude.

← N.A.A.W.

XANDER

Weak, yo. WEAK!

REESE

I know! I'm sorry!

So Dad started marching us up Broadway, back toward where I last saw James. And he was all, "If you were James, where would you go?"

XANDER

And I's all, "Prison." Cause J-Mo be seriously headed for jail if he don't check himself.

And Big Daddy Tapper was all, "We'll look there later."

WYATT

Then I went, "Dunkin' Donuts!"

And your dad was like, "Does James like donuts?"

And I was like, "I dunno—but there's a Dunkin' Donuts right over there. And we can buy a donut and pretend it's a Cronut!"

REESE

Which was a sweet idea. Because even though I ate the Cronut, I'd kept the box.

So we basically ran in and bought the donut before Dad could even argue with us.

We got a strawberry glazed, 'cause it looked like the Cronut I'd eaten, except it was a little too oval-ish. So I chewed around the edges to make it look more Cronut-y.

Then we put it in the box. Although I'd been carrying the Calvin head around in

there, so the box was, like, kind of soggy
from the skruzzy subway water.

A.B.N.Q.A.A.W.—
Almost (But Not Quite)
An Actual Word

CLAUDIA

Just please tell me nobody ever put
that half-eaten donut back in their mouth
after it had been sitting in that scuzzy box.

this is just WAY
BEYOND DISGUSTING

A.A.W.
(An Actual word)

REESE

No comment.

Anyway, after we got the replacement
Cronut, Dad was like, "Check your email—
maybe James wrote back!"

And I was like, "Dad, there's no way...
ohmygosh, he actually did."

JAMES (email to Reese)

✕ ─ ✛   RE: JAMES WHERE R U???????

✕ ← ← → ✉

From: i_m_batman_4realz@yahoo.com
To: skronkmonster@gmail.com
Date: 10/25/14 1:02:33 PM EDT
Subject: RE: JAMES WHERE R U???????

On October 25, 2014 at 12:54 PM, Reese Tapper
<skronkmonster@gmail.com> wrote:
MY DAD IS SUPER WORRIED PLZ CHECK IN
W HIM ~~~~~~~~

Im all alone n scared pls come get me corner of
Flatbush and Atlantic

REESE

I showed the email to Dad, and he was
like, "Flatbush and Atlantic? How did he get
all the way to Brooklyn?"

And then Dad was like, "We have to go
get him."

And the rest of us were like, "But then

we'll never win the scavenger hunt! There's only a few hours left!"

WYATT

Then your dad was all, "Guys, I'm going to be completely honest with you: there's ALREADY no way you're going to win. It's after 1:00pm, and all you've got is a taxi receipt, some mangled legs in front of the Statue of Liberty, and a half-eaten donut.

"You're getting CRUSHED. Now, come with me and we'll go get James, so at least everybody can get home in one piece."

XANDER

That was harsh, yo. Big Daddy Tapper done showed us the back of his hand with that speech.

But I was aaiite with it. 'Cause I was cookin' up a secret plan to win.

REESE

Xander asked my dad if the three of us could take a cab back to his place—which was just a couple blocks from Culvert Prep—and wait there while Dad went to Brooklyn to get James.

Wyatt and I were like, "Why do you want to go to your place?"

And Xander was all, "Secret plan, yo."

And we were like, "What secret plan?"

And he was like, "Two words: Photoshop."

CLAUDIA

"Photoshop" is one word.

REESE

Seriously? It's not, like, "photo" and "shop"?

CLAUDIA

No. It's just "Photoshop."

list of things
Xander doesn't
know is VERY
VERY LONG
↓

REESE

Oh. I don't think Xander knows that. Anyway, Dad wasn't too hot on the idea of us splitting up again. But we swore up and down we'd go straight to Xander's and not leave there for any reason, except maybe if his apartment was on fire.

Then Dad was like, "WHY would Xander's apartment be on fire?"

And we were like, "There won't be a fire! It was just an example!"

And he was like, "PROMISE me you're not
going to light anything on fire."

And we were like, "OF COURSE NOT!"

So finally, he put us in a cab *more bad
judgment by Dad (but did not actually result in fire)*
uptown and then headed to Brooklyn
to find James.

I probably should have reminded Dad
that James is a huge liar, so there was a
good chance he wasn't really in Brooklyn.
But I was so psyched to find out about
Xander's secret plan that I just kind of
forgot.

So that was my bad.

CHAPTER 20
PARVATI GETS A
LITTLE TOO LOUD

CLAUDIA

It turns out there's a downside to being as famous as Deondra, which is that whenever you're at home, shifty-looking guys with huge cameras will hang around outside your apartment to snap pictures and/or follow you when you leave.

shifty-looking
guys with cameras
(aka paparazzi)

The official word for them is "paparazzi," which I think means "annoying photographer" in Italian. There were four of them hanging around outside Deondra's building when we got there. I don't think

any of them were actually Italian, but one
was French. And even though he was shifty-
looking, he turned out to be very cool.

JENS

The French one was a good guy, for sure.

Jacques
(French
paparazzo)

"o" at end is
singular
(I looked it up)

scar on
forearm from
when movie
star bit him
(see p. 190)

CLAUDIA

His name was Jacques. When Jens and I
started hanging out in front of the building,
he said, "You look for Deondra?"

I said, "Yes! Do you know if she's inside?"

Jacques said, "Think so. Assistant came
and walked dog. So dog is home. Usually, if
dog is home, so is Deondra."

"What kind of dog is it?" I asked him.

"Rottweiler," he said. Which made sense. If a bunch of shifty-looking guys were constantly hanging around outside my apartment, I'd get a Rottweiler, too.

Rottweiler: excellent dog for celebrities with paparazzi problem

Then he said, "You want to meet her?"

I said, "Not exactly...We just need a picture of her kissing this—" and I showed him our Calvin the Cat. He gave us a weird look, so we explained about the scavenger hunt.

JENS

I asked the French guy, "Do you think she will do this for us?"

And he said, "Maybe. For big star, she

is pretty cool. But you should hope dog is
not with her."

So I said, "The dog is not cool also?"

And he said, "The dog is a real ———."
Which is a word I did not know in
English.

*can't use
actual word
(b/c filthy)*

Then he thought some more and
said, "But maybe dog just don't like
photographers."

CLAUDIA

For a while after that, not much
happened, except that Jacques told us
paparazzi stories. Some of them were pretty
crazy. At one point, he showed us a scar
on his forearm that he said he got when
a very famous movie star bit him outside
a restaurant.

*Dad says I can't print
name or I will get sued.*

I'm not 100% sure that was true,
but the scar was definitely bite-shaped.
And considering what I've read online
about that particular movie star, it seems
believable.

Then the gate went up at the entrance
to Deondra's building's parking garage, and
a big SUV came out.

big SUV (not Deondra's)
(but looked just like this)

All the paparazzi suddenly ran to their vehicles—two of them had motorcycles, one was on a mountain bike, and Jacques was riding a Vespa scooter—and zoomed off to follow the SUV.

"Where are they going?" we yelled at him.

"Don't know!" he yelled back. But before he scootered off, he gave us his business card and told us if we texted him our number, he'd text back and let us know where Deondra ended up.

JACQUES DANTON

PHOTOGRAPHY / PHOTOGRAPHIE

PARIS: +33
NEW YORK: (917)
ClickChat: com

U.S. number (pretty sure it is crazy expensive to text someone in France)

So we texted the number on his card, and five minutes later, he texted back.

TEXT MESSAGES (Claudia and shifty-but-cool French guy)

> Hi, Jacques! I am the Deondra fan you just met. If you could text me her location, that would be amazingly awesome, and I would hugely appreciate it.

> Zoso in West Village

CLAUDIA

I had no idea what Zoso was, so I googled it.

PARVATI

I can NOT believe you never heard of Zoso. It's, like, THE most happening restaurant in all of Manhattan.

CLAUDIA

Had you ever been there?

PARVATI

Of course not! It's, like, impossible to

get a table if you're a normal human being.
You have to be either famous or rich or both.

CLAUDIA

Zoso is so exclusive it doesn't even have
a website, so we had to get the exact location
(Grove Street) from an OMG Celebrities In The
Wild! story about a movie star who threw up on
a parked car outside the front door.

NOT same movie star who bit Jacques

We got in a cab—which cost me almost all
the cash I had, but I didn't want to take any
chances—and drove to Grove Street, which is
one of those totally cute West Village side
streets that looks like a movie set.

totally cute West Village side street (Grove)

Along the way, I called Parvati—who was still in line for the FAO Schwarz floor piano—because this was a huge moment for Team Melting Pot. And I wanted to congratulate her for the amazing detective work.

Unfortunately, calling Parvati turned out to be an epic mistake.

PARVATI

Can I just say, what happened was NOT my fault?

CARMEN

How was it not your fault? You screamed, "CLAUDIA FOUND DEONDRA! SHE'S EATING BRUNCH AT ZOSO!" Like, so loud the entire store heard it.

PARVATI

You're the one who asked me why I was jumping up and down!

CARMEN

I didn't know you were going to scream highly sensitive information at the top of your lungs! ESPECIALLY when Colin Hartley was standing two feet away from us!

PARVATI

I'm sorry, but if YOU had spent your entire life worshiping Deondra and everything she does? You'd go a little mental when you found out where she was having brunch, too.

Speaking of mental—Colin posting that on ClickChat was, like, the world's dumbest move. It's one thing to, like, go down to Zoso and get a Deondra pic yourself.

But telling EVERYONE in the hunt where she is? Totally ridic.

CLAUDIA

Zoso didn't have a sign or menu or anything out front, so when we got to Grove Street, we wouldn't have known where it was if it hadn't been for all the paparazzi standing across the street.

Zoso
(so trendy you
can't even tell
it's a restaurant)
(except for Board of
Health grade in window)

front door
(hidden under stairs)

We thanked Jacques for hooking us up. Then we tried to go inside. But we didn't get more than a foot in the door when the hosts (or maitre d's, or front door people, or whatever you call them) stopped us. They were a super-skinny tall guy with a crazy expensive haircut and an even skinnier/taller/more-expensive-haircut blond woman, both dressed in matching black turtlenecks.

artist's re-creation of Zoso hosts (very skinny and mean)

JENS

The man said, "May I help you?" But the way he said it, he did not really want to help.

And when you said, "A table for two, please?"
the woman made a funny sound in her nose.

CLAUDIA

They were complete snobs. And right after
they told us there weren't any tables, this
gigantic bouncer suddenly appeared.

JENS

I think the bouncer was there the whole
time. Only before he moved, I thought he was
furniture. Like a bookcase.

CLAUDIA

I have actually never seen a human being
that large. I have no idea how they found a
turtleneck in his size.

artist's re-creation
of Zoso bouncer
(NOT skinny but
def mean)

Two seconds later, we were back on the street. But we figured we didn't actually have to get inside—all we had to do was wait for Deondra to finish eating brunch, then beg her for a photo with the Calvin when she left.

So we sat down on the steps of a brownstone two doors down and started to wait.

That's when I checked ClickChat and realized things were about to get crazy.

CLICKCHAT POSTS ON "CULVERT PREP SCAVENGER HUNT" WALL

Daniella R. (The Fierceness)

daniR But if its 4 inches cant we get at least 2 pts???

Akash CzarOfTheHunt No partial credit. A three-inch or smaller Empire State Building is 4 points. Anything else is zero points.

Colin (Gingivitis) HartAttack01 DEONDRA SIGHTING AT ZOZO

daniR WHAT?????!!!!!

daniR What is ZOZO?

Natasha (Wut Ups) tasha_sez Do u mean Zoso? The restaurant?

HartAttack01 Y

CzarOfTheHunt Deondra item is a JOKE! Get on with your lives, people.

HartAttack01 Yah but its on the list. So if we get pic its 500 pts. Rt?

HartAttack01 Right? 500 pts for Deondra kissing Clavin

HartAttack01 Right, Akash???

HartAttack01 RIGHT??????

CzarOfTheHunt Hang on checking w Mrs Bevan

CzarOfTheHunt Technically that is correct

tasha_sez OMG I m going to Zoso now. Grove Street in W Village

HartAttack01 Dont bother JKopp is almost there and he will get 500 pts before u

tasha_sez Who cares whose first? We can ALL get 500 pts

AidanTheGrif heading there stat

numbah_tehn HOLLA DAT

BritSeavs THIS IS AMAZING!!!!

Aidan (Killaz)

Tucker (Wolves)

Brittany (The Fierceness)

CLAUDIA

The first thing I saw when I looked up from my phone was Josh Koppelman from Gingivitis, running full speed down Grove Street toward us.

When he stopped and asked where Zoso was, Jens and I played dumb. But he figured it out and barged right in.

Five seconds later, he barged right back out again. When he did, he looked pretty freaked out. Probably because of the bouncer.

JENS

Then the big eighth grade boy, Josh,

stands between us and restaurant. So if
Deondra comes, he is first.

CLAUDIA

This seemed like a problem.

But pretty soon, we had MUCH bigger
problems. Because a minute later, Ella
Daniels from The Fierceness came running
up the street.

Natasha Minello from The Wut Ups was
right behind her.

Then Luke Schwartz from Team Awesome
showed up.

Followed by Dimitri and Toby from The
Knights Who Say Ni.

Then a whole flood of kids from
Killaz...Cutsies!...JBTW...Lords Of The
UES...Fire Team Four...The Dark Knights...
Wolves...and pretty much every other team
in the scavenger hunt.

Plus a bunch of tourists and random
people who saw the crowd and figured
something must be happening, so they should
stand around and watch it happen.

Within ten minutes, there were so many
people crowding around the entrance of Zoso

that cars were having trouble driving up the
street.

Then Athena Cohen and her mom showed up,
and the trouble really started.

Satan's Town Car
(actually Athena's)
(not same car that she used)
(but close enough)

CHAPTER 21
NIGHTMARE ON GROVE STREET

CLAUDIA

I knew it was Athena and her mom as soon as I saw their stupid chauffeur-driven Town Car turn the corner at the end of the block.

It stopped right in front of Zoso, and there was such a huge crowd that when their driver opened the door for Athena and her mom, it looked like they were making a grand entrance at a movie premiere.

The enormous bouncer guy was outside by now, guarding the front door. And the skinny hosts were sort of cowering behind him. I think because the size of the crowd was freaking them out.

enormous bouncer guy
(did NOT like having
his pic taken)

Athena and her mom headed straight
for the door, and for a second I got all
excited, because I figured they were going
to get turned away like the rest of us, and
it would be totally humiliating.

So what happened next was a huge and
terrible shock.

JENS

I think maybe Athena's mom eats at Zoso
a lot. Because host guy made a big smile and
said, "SO GREAT TO SEE YOU AGAIN!"

Then the giant man opens the door so
they can go inside.

When he did that, the whole crowd made
the noise—how do you say it? "Gapped"?

*Jens's English =
not perfect
(but adorable)*

CLAUDIA

"Gasped." Everybody gasped.

JENS

Yes. And then Athena made a wave. And
everybody was angry.

CLAUDIA

Right before she disappeared inside,
Athena turned and waved to all of us.

It was basically Athena's way of saying, "HA-HA-HA, MY PARENTS ARE SO RICH AND HOOKED UP THAT WE CAN GET A TABLE AT ZOSO WHILE THE REST OF YOU WAIT OUTSIDE LIKE PEASANTS."

It was the most evil, smug wave I have ever seen in my life.

Everybody else thought so, too.

JOSH KOPPELMAN, Gingivitis team member

I was RIPPED when she did that. What's that girl's name? Athena? Total brat.

NATASHA MINELLO, The Wut Ups team member

I pretty much wanted to strangle her.

LUKE SCHWARTZ, Team Awesome

If I had to describe my feelings at that moment in, like, two words? They would be "blind rage."

CLAUDIA

But as mad as everybody was, it's VERY important to understand this: no matter what the stupid *New York Star* said, we did NOT actually start a riot.

The absolutely closest we ever came was maybe halfway to a riot. That was right

after Athena did her little wave, and
this angry rumble went through the crowd.
And people kinda/sorta surged toward
the door.

But then the bouncer put his hands up
and went, "YO! BACK THE CUSS UP!" NOTE: not the
actual word he used

And when he said that, we all backed
the cuss up. Because he was very large, and
we respected his authority.

All things considered, the whole crowd
was actually very well behaved.

So there was no reason for the police
to even show up. Let alone six of them.

AKASH

You are seriously lucky Mrs. Bevan
didn't find out about the cops showing up
until that reporter called her, like, four
hours later.

CLAUDIA

Do NOT even get me started about that
reporter. Almost everything in his article
was a huge lie. I am not even going to
reprint the whole thing, because it was so
ridiculous. But for the record, here's the
top part:

SCHOOLKID SCAVENGERS RUN RIOT
Private School Kids, Parents In Fundraiser Fracas

civil war
gay rights →

ha-ha-ha
(NOT
funny) →

New York City's seen the Draft Riots, the Stonewall Riots…and now the Tween Riot.

On Saturday afternoon, a mob of middle schoolers from one of NYC's most elite private schools descended on Zoso in the West Village.

set fire to a garbage can, and a motorist trying to navigate the clogged street was reportedly pulled from his vehicle by a pack of pubescent lacrosse players chanting "We want assassination!,"

"Kill someone!," and other threats.

front-row seats at MSG!" gushed sixth grader Dimitri Sharansky. "I'd totally trample over people for that."

"We all would," added his classmate Toby Zimmerman. "People at Culvert Pre are super-competitive.

Not. True. At. All. Except for what
Toby said about people at Culvert being
super-competitive.

AKASH

Are you SURE none of it was true? Like,
nobody set fire to a garbage can?

CLAUDIA

No! I think one of the paparazzi threw
away a match, and it set fire to a napkin or
something. But that was it.

AKASH

Nobody pulled a guy out of his car?

CLAUDIA

No! That guy got out voluntarily to yell at everybody for blocking the street.

And he was kind of a jerk about it, so a couple of the eighth grade boys got a little lippy with him.

But then he just called them punks and drove off.

AKASH

And they weren't chanting "We want assassination!"?

CLAUDIA

Of course not! It was "We want A RESERVATION!"

AKASH

How about "Kill someone!"? I heard people were going, "What do we want? To kill someone!"

CLAUDIA

That is ridiculous. They were going, "What do we want? A KALE SALAD! When do we want it? Now!"

Because supposedly the kale salad is Zoso's signature dish. And I guess the Gingivitis guys thought they were being hilarious by chanting that.

kale salad
(not actual Zoso salad)
(but prob like this one)
(but might not have apples)

AKASH

So if it was never an actual riot, why did the cops show up?

CLAUDIA

I seriously do not know. Except I think the skinny guy in the turtleneck must have called them.

And anyway, by the time the cops got there, it was basically over. Because the skinny guy had come out and yelled, "DEONDRA HAS LEFT THE BUILDING! SHE WENT OUT THE BACK DOOR."

At first, nobody believed him. But then we realized the paparazzi were all gone, so he must've been telling the truth.

Plus, by then Athena had posted her totally obnoxious message on the ClickChat wall. Which was basically the final nail in the coffin.

CLICKCHAT POSTS ON "CULVERT PREP SCAVENGER HUNT" WALL

Athena (evil)

goddessgurrl Just got THE CUTEST PIC of Deondra with Calvin the Cat. Will post right after I cash it in for 500 pts!

goddessgurrl She is just the best. SO nice! Sorry you all missed her. She went out back door to avoid the crowd.

goddessgurrl BTW kale salad is to die for. Don't think I can finish mine, tho. Who wants my doggy bag?

CLAUDIA

Jens and I were walking away when Parvati, Carmen, and my mom showed up.

CARMEN

I have never seen you that sad in your entire life. It was even worse than that time you sprained your ankle in gym class.

volleyball = more dangerous than it looks

CLAUDIA

It actually hurt worse than when I sprained my ankle.

It was a different kind of hurt. But it was definitely worse.

PARVATI

I still can't believe I missed it. Like, I know nobody except Athena actually SAW Deondra. But it still would've been an honor just to be on the same block as my idol.

CLAUDIA

By this point, it was almost 3:00. And since we knew evil had triumphed, there didn't seem to be any point in killing ourselves to get a few more items before the hunt ended at 4:00.

So we ate an incredibly depressing lunch at a 99-cent pizza place (4 points. Yay.), then took the subway back uptown.

sarcastic "yay"

BTW, you get what you pay for with 99-cent pizza. The reason it's so cheap is because it has about 10 cents' worth of cheese and 5 cents' worth of tomato sauce. Which is not actually enough to cover the

whole slice. So it's really like eating
pizza-flavored crust.

99-CENT PIZZA

sauce-related stain (not actual sauce)

supposedly cheese

not cheese

looks like cheese (but isn't)

JENS

    Please say thank you again to your
mother for buying the lunch.

CLAUDIA

    It was only $3.96 for all four of us.
But okay.

(no bevs)

CHAPTER 22
BEAST SQUAD: THE
FINAL HUMILIATION

CLAUDIA

At this point, things looked grim for anybody who wasn't a Fembot.

But they were especially grim for Beast Squad.

Three-fourths of Reese's team (James Mantolini was still missing in action) were holed up in Xander's Park Avenue apartment, working on his "secret plan"—which was to Photoshop their Calvin onto pictures they'd downloaded from the Internet.

This would've been a real long shot EVEN IF they were experts at using Photoshop.

But they were definitely not experts.

And their Calvin was just beyond disgusting.

REESE

We tried to wash the Calvin off in the kitchen sink, but we couldn't really get the

stains out. He didn't smell as bad after we
washed him, though, so it wasn't a total fail.

Then we were going to sew his legs
back on and staple his head shut. But none
of us could sew, and we couldn't get the
stapler to work. So we used Scotch tape.
Which didn't really stick. So we just
kind of stacked his parts together
and took a pic.

Then we started Photoshopping the pic.
But first, Xander and Wyatt got in a big
fight over who was going to use the mouse.

WYATT

No offense to Xander? But he did NOT know what he was doing. I mean, it's not like I'm some kind of Photoshop expert. But at least I've used it before. I don't think Xander had ever even opened it.

XANDER

Peep this, yo: MY idea. MY Photoshop. MY hand on the mouse.
Also, MY Cheetos.

WYATT

Once he started licking the Cheeto dust off his fingers and, like, getting wet clumps of Cheeto gunk all over the mouse? I was like, "Never mind. 'Cause there's no way I'm touching that now."

REESE

We started with a Deondra photo, because, duh, 500 points.
But it turned out to be super hard. It took us forever just to find a picture of Deondra kissing somebody. And swapping in the Calvin was even harder.

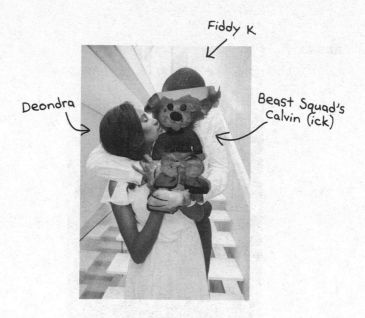

Fiddy K

Deondra

Beast Squad's
Calvin (ick)

CLAUDIA

That might be the saddest thing I have
ever seen in my life.

Except for all your other fake photos.

REESE

They weren't THAT bad.

WYATT

They were terrible. After I saw how bad
the Deondra pic came out, I basically gave
up and just played Xbox while Xander and
Reese worked on the other ones.

REESE

I thought the Flubby one was good.

CLAUDIA

Except you made the Calvin look ten feet tall. When he's really nine inches.

WYATT

Seriously. He was, like, Godzilla Calvin rampaging through Times Square.

REESE

No way! He didn't look THAT big. I mean, if anything was Godzilla Calvin, it was the one on the Cyclone.

WYATT

That one was crazy. It was like the Calvin was about to swallow the roller coaster.

REESE

The Yankee Stadium one was okay.

CLAUDIA

That depends on what your definition of "okay" is.

WYATT

It looked like a Calvin superhero flying over the stadium. If the superhero had, like, just gotten sucked through a jet engine.

REESE

We basically ran out of time on that one. Because Dad called and was like, "It's almost four o'clock—meet me back at Culvert Prep!"

I went, "Did you find James?"

And there was this big sigh from Dad. And he was like, "No...Is there something wrong with that kid?"

And I was like, "Totally. Didn't I tell you that?"

And Dad was like, "No, you didn't."

So I said I was sorry for not giving him a heads up about James before he went all the way to Brooklyn.

And he was like, "Brooklyn was only half of it. I'm coming back from Queens."

JAMES AND DAD (email exchanges)

⊗ ⊖ ⊕   RE: I AM COMING TO GET YOU
✕ ← ⇐ → ✉
From: i_m_batman_4realz@yahoo.com
To: eric.steven.tapper@gmail.com
Date: 10/25/14 1:23:16 PM EDT
Subject: RE: I AM COMING TO GET YOU

On October 25, 2014 at 1:14 PM, Eric Tapper
<eric.steven.tapper@gmail.com> wrote:

James, this is Reese's father. Are you still at
the corner of Flatbush and Atlantic? If so, stay
there—I will come get you. Either way, text me at
~~911-555-5510~~ASAP and let me know where
you are.

Ok just please hurry some guys from a cult want me to go
with them in their van

✕ ← ⇐ → ✉

FROM: i_m_batman_4realz@yahoo.com
TO: eric.steven.tapper@gmail.com
DATE: 10/25/14 1:42:11 PM EDT
SUBJECT: RE: WHERE ARE YOU?

On October 25, 2014 at 1:37 PM, Eric Tapper
<eric.steven.tapper@gmail.com> wrote:

I'm at Flatbush and Atlantic. Are you here?
Please call/text me at ~~911-555-5510~~ ASAP

Yeah sorry guys from cult offered me candy so I went
with them. Driving to Queens in their van to play
Lazer Tag.

Flatbush and Atlantic
(James was never
actually here)

⊗ ⊖ ⊕   RE: PLEASE BE AT CULVERT PREP...

✕ ← ⇐ → ✉

FROM: i_m_batman_4realz@yahoo.com

TO: eric.steven.tapper@gmail.com

DATE: 10/25/14 1:52:54 PM EDT

SUBJECT: RE: PLEASE BE AT CULVERT PREP BY 4:00PM

On October 25, 2014 at 1:47 PM, Eric Tapper
<eric.steven.tapper@gmail.com> wrote:
I have begun to suspect you are not being completely
serious. Just please get back to Culvert Prep by 4:00,
as I am personally responsible for your well-being.

Sorry. I was kidding about the cult but not the guys in the van.
When we got to Lazer Tag place, they took all my money and
drove off. Can you come get me? I have no way to get home
and 3% left on phone battery. 47th Ave and Van Dam

FROM: i_m_batman_4realz@yahoo.com

TO: eric.steven.tapper@gmail.com

DATE: 10/25/14 2:37:54 PM EDT

SUBJECT: RE: RE: RE: PLEASE BE AT CULVERT PREP BY 4:00PM

> On October 25, 2014 at 2:36 PM, Eric Tapper <eric.steven.tapper@gmail.com> wrote:
>
> I am standing outside Laser Tag place and starting to get very angry. The guys in the van didn't exist, did they?
>
> I'M COMING! Be there in 5 min. 1% of battery left DON'T LEAVE!

Laser Tag place
(James was never
here, either)

FROM: i_m_batman_4realz@yahoo.com
TO: eric.steven.tapper@gmail.com
DATE: 10/25/14 2:53:02 PM EDT
SUBJECT: RE: RE: RE: RE: RE: PLEASE BE AT CULVERT PREP BY 4:00PM

> On October 25, 2014 at 2:45 PM, Eric Tapper
> <eric.steven.tapper@gmail.com> wrote:
> James, are you aware of just how uncool this is?
> I'm afraid I'm going to have to call your parents.

OK but it'll probably just go to voice mail.

CHAPTER 23
DAD GETS A SERIOUS
TALKING TO

CLAUDIA

When we showed up at the Culvert Prep
auditorium around 3:50, Akash and Mrs. Bevan
were at a table on stage, adding up points
for the teams that had come back early.

About thirty kids were already there, and
the mood was ugly. When the Fembots showed up—
Athena and her mom swaggering down the aisle
like Princess Evil and The Ice Queen, with
Ling/Meredith/Clarissa trailing after them
like wicked stepsisters—a few people actually
booed them.

CARMEN

Personally, I really appreciated the
booing. It was nice to know that even if the
Fembots had won, everybody hated them for it.

CLAUDIA

This cheered me up, too. But only a little.
Then Team Melting Pot went up and got our
items counted. Akash and Mrs. Bevan weren't

announcing official scores yet,
but we figured we had 76 points: not bad,
but definitely not enough to beat the
Fembots even without their stupid 500-point
Deondra photo.

misc. stuff
Carmen/Parvati/Mom
got while Jens and
I were stalking
Deondra

On the other hand, when you multiplied
the 76 points by all our pledges, they
amounted to $436.20, all of which went to
the Manhattan Food Bank. Which was awesome.

So I tried to focus on that instead
of the fact that the Fembots were going to
win and life was totally unfair and I had
created a scavenger hunt monster.

Then my dad showed up with three-
fourths of Beast Squad, and they went up to
get their items counted.

REESE

We were, like, kind of worried and kind
of hopeful. Because the Photoshop stuff
seemed like a long shot.

But we still had a 30-point Cronut!
Sort of. not really

WYATT

The thing was, it was almost four o'clock.
So we knew if James didn't show up in, like,
five minutes, we'd get disqualified.

Your dad seemed pretty stressed about
that. Not the getting disqualified part
so much as the part where he lost a whole
person.

AKASH

I just have to say—thank Shiva that
Reese and his moron friends exist. Because
I'd just spent six straight hours alone with
Mrs. Bevan, who was being a total stressball
about everything. So I desperately needed
a laugh.

And, oh, man, did they give me one.

CLAUDIA

The first thing Reese did was hand
Akash this soggy yellow box from the Cronut
bakery. As soon as Akash opened the box, he
started laughing.

AKASH

They've got this Dominique Ansel box—
which they must've, like, dropped in a sewer,
because it's got all these weird stains on it.
And it seriously does NOT smell good.

And I look inside, and there's this
strawberry frosted donut—which I'm almost
100% sure was from Dunkin' Donuts—that
they've, like, nibbled on around the edges
so it's sort of vaguely Cronut-shaped.

But really, all it looked like was a
totally disgusting, half-eaten donut. With
sprinkles.

And I said, "What the heck is this?"

REESE

And I was like, "It's...aaaaa...Cronut?"
Which was tough. Because I am, like, NOT a
good liar. True. Reese is a TERRIBLE liar

AKASH

It was completely insane. I mean, HELLO? I'm a Cronut connoisseur! I know my Cronuts.

Even Mrs. Bevan, who was a total Cronut virgin, was like, "I REALLY don't think that's a Cronut."

REESE

So I was like, "The thing is...we HAD a Cronut. But I ate it."

AKASH

At this point, I'm laughing too hard to talk. But Mrs. Bevan goes, "Why did you eat the Cronut?"

REESE

And I was like, "'Cause James and I were trapped in a truck."

And she was like, "HOW did you get trapped in a truck?"

And I was like, "We were getting chased by soccer hooligans. 'Cause we were in this bar, and..."

WYATT

When Reese said "bar," Mrs. Bevan's

eyes, like, bulged out of her skull.

And she turned to your dad. Who, like, could NOT have looked more worried.

XANDER ← Xander's name for Vice Principal Bevan (I think)

I could see V-Bevs fixing to come down HARD on that.

So I was all, "Yo, we gots to change the subject STAT!" And I whipped out dem pics.

AKASH

So that Xander idiot shoves his phone in my face and goes, "YO, PEEP THESE PICS!"

And I got one look at...oh, man...I guess it was their Calvin, but it looked like a bear had eaten it and then pooped it back out again—and they'd Photoshopped it so it was, like, flying over Yankee Stadium....

And I just lost it.

CLAUDIA

Akash basically had an uncontrollable
laughing fit on stage. He was doubled over
in his chair, red in the face.

But Mrs. Bevan was definitely not
laughing.

REESE

Mrs. Bevan was all, "Mr. Tapper, can I
speak with you privately?"

And she took Dad over to the side of the
stage and basically started chewing him out.

I couldn't hear everything they said.
But at some point, it stopped being about
the bar and started being about how Dad lost
James. Like, I heard her go, "Did he have a
cell phone?" And "WHERE is the last place
you saw him?"

CLAUDIA

It's possible Mrs. Bevan would STILL
be standing on that stage yelling at my dad
if James Mantolini hadn't burst into the
auditorium just then. He was all sweaty and
out of breath, and he yelled "THREE FIFTY-
NINE!" (i.e., 1 minute before 4:00pm deadline)

Then he collapsed. But not the serious kind of collapsed. More like a fake, drama-queening, just-finished-running-a-marathon collapse.

So Mrs. Bevan called James up to the stage, and after she'd interrogated him—and he showed her and Akash something on his phone—she told Beast Squad to go sit down.

REESE

We sat down, and we were all like, "James, where were you?" And "What's on your phone?"

And James was like, "No comment."

JAMES

I like to keep things on a need-to-know basis. And they did not need to know.

CLAUDIA

The fact that James wasn't dead ← (or missing body parts) basically got Dad off the hook with Mrs. Bevan.

But not with Mom. Who spent the rest of the weekend chewing him out for A) being the world's worst chaperone, and B) lying to her about it.

In fact, she still hasn't really gotten over it:

MOM AND DAD (text messages)

2 WEEKS AFTER SCAVENGER HUNT:

DAD → Taking Reese's soccer team out for pizza after game

TRY NOT TO LOSE ANY OF THEM ← MOM

3 WEEKS AFTER SCAVENGER HUNT:

At fish counter. Salmon looks better than tuna. Should I get that for dinner?

How do I know you're not lying to me about the salmon?

Guy at fish counter will back me up

HOW MANY LIES HAVE YOU TOLD THE GUY AT THE FISH COUNTER, ERIC?

Working late tonight

Prove it

Seriously?

Yes. Text a pic of you at office holding copy of today's newspaper

Also need sworn affidavits from co-workers

Will this joke ever get old for you?

Trust can't be given, Eric. It must be earned.

CHAPTER 24
PHOTO FINISH

CLAUDIA

By the time Beast Squad got off the stage, it was after 4:00, so Akash and Mrs. Bevan closed the auditorium door and took attendance.

Six teams got disqualified for missing players. My guess is the absent kids just couldn't bear to watch the Fembots win front-row MSG tickets for being completely evil.

PARVATI

Can I just say, I kind of don't blame the kids who skipped it? I mean, everybody was BEYOND sure the Fembots were going to win.

And the whole time the points were getting added up, Athena Cohen would NOT stop rubbing it in.

CARMEN

Athena was just off-the-charts annoying. She kept making these loud, totally obnoxious comments to the other Fembots, like "I don't know if we should use the front-row seats on a Deondra concert. I mean, I JUST SAW her from, like, two feet away. Too bad nobody else did...."

CLAUDIA

Finally, Mrs. Bevan got up to announce the winners.

First, she thanked everybody for participating and reminded us again that the whole scavenger hunt was for charity, and the truly important thing was that we all helped raise a lot of money for the Manhattan Food Bank.

I am very proud to say there was a huge round of applause for that.

Then she said, "Before I announce the top three finishers, remember—no matter how many points you got, EVERYBODY'S a winner."

And Athena Cohen went, "But especially us!" loud enough that even Mrs. Bevan heard her.

Ordinarily, this is the kind of behavior that'd make Mrs. Bevan stop everything for a "teachable moment" about not being a horrible person. "teachable moment" = 5-minute lecture (at least)

So it was kind of a surprise when she just paused for a second and bit her lip like she was trying not to smile.

And it was an ABSOLUTELY ENORMOUSLY HUGE SURPRISE when she said, "In third place: Goddesses, Inc.!"

For about two seconds, the whole auditorium was stunned into silence.

Then there was laughing.

Followed by cheering.

CARMEN

All I can say is, the Fembots only getting third place was the greatest moment in the history of anything. Anywhere. Ever. It was SO sweet.

PARVATI

I seriously almost fainted.

Actually, I think I DID faint. For like a second.

REESE

It was pretty awesome. I mean, ordinarily, I don't have a problem with Athena and Ling and those girls. But the way they were trash-talking everybody was pretty uncool. So they totally deserved it.

CLAUDIA

At first, the Fembots looked like they were in shock. Then they got angry.

Then Mrs. Bevan held up one of the pencil cases and called out, "Come on up, girls!"

Culvert Prep pencil case (zipper usually breaks after 5+ uses) (also plastic very cheap and can cause skin rash)

This was followed by a little muttering argument between Athena and her mom, because Athena clearly did NOT want to go up on stage.

But eventually, Mrs. Cohen marched them all up there.

The absolutely best thing about the scavenger hunt was raising all that money for the Manhattan Food Bank.

But the second-best thing was DEFINITELY
the look on Athena Cohen's face when Mrs.
Bevan handed her a ten-cent pencil case in *not actual*
exchange for the gazillion dollars she'd *amount*
(probably
just spent trying to buy her way to victory. *more like*

As the Fembots skulked back to their *high $100s/*
low $1,000s)
seats, Parvati nudged me and went, "Who do
you think got the other two Deondra pics?"

I figured it must be somebody whose
parents were either super-rich or hooked up,
because they were the only people who'd have
access to Deondra.

So it was a pretty huge surprise when
Mrs. Bevan said, "In second place...the
Avada Kedavras!"

In all honesty, I was very happy for
Kalisha and her team. Even if all they got
was a Starbucks gift certificate.

PARVATI

You didn't act like you were happy for
them.

CLAUDIA

Maybe because you kept elbowing me in
the ribs and muttering, "See? SEE?"

PARVATI

I was just saying—if we had Kalisha on our team, that could've been us.

CARMEN

Totally. She masterminded that team.

CLAUDIA

Whatever! It's not like Kalisha actually won the whole thing.

PARVATI

She SHOULD have.

CARMEN

No kidding! I'm still in shock over who won.

CLAUDIA

We all are.

I seriously do not know how to explain this. So I'm just going to use Mrs. Bevan's exact words:

"The winners of the First Annual Culvert Prep Middle School Scavenger Hunt For Charity: BEAST SQUAD!"

CHAPTER 25
SHOCK AND AWE
(AND LAWSUITS)

REESE

WHOOOOOOOO! WHOOOOOOOO!
WHOOOOOOOOOOOOOOOOOOOOOOOOOOOOOO!

WYATT

Do you believe in miracles? DO YOU
BELIEVE IN MIRACLES?

XANDER

AWWWWW YEAH!
SECRET PLAN, BABY!

CLAUDIA

Okay, THAT is ridiculous. Beast Squad's
victory had absolutely NOTHING to do with
Xander's incredibly lame Photoshopping.

In fact, I still think they should've
gotten disqualified for trying to cheat.

AKASH

It's a fair argument. But I don't think
you can disqualify somebody for trying

to cheat in a way that's so completely incompetent it wouldn't fool a dead man.

And credit where credit is due: James Mantolini delivered the goods.

JAMES

I think my work speaks for itself.

CLAUDIA

Let me back up a little and try to explain what happened at the end, because it is very confusing. also COMPLETELY INSANE

Mrs. Bevan had barely finished handing Reese and his idiot friends their front-row tickets to Madison Square Garden when Athena's mom rushed the stage to demand a recount.

I was pretty much in shock—actually, everyone in the room was pretty much in shock—but when I saw Mrs. Cohen make her move, I knew there was going to be a fight.

And I decided that, as the founder and co-organizer of the scavenger hunt, I should be present for it. So I ran up on stage myself.

Eventually, so did half the school. It was basically chaos.

REESE

I didn't even realize it was Athena's mom at first. All I knew was, suddenly there was this lady on stage yelling, "HAVE THESE RESULTS BEEN AUDITED?!"

And I was like, "I do NOT know what that word means. But I'm going to stick my front-row ticket in my pants so nobody can take it from me." *eeeeew*

WYATT

Mrs. Cohen was going, "HOW ON EARTH DID THOSE BOYS WIN?"

And I was like, "Yeah—how DID we win?"

Because once I stopped to think about it, it kind of didn't make sense.

AKASH

I'm a professional, okay? The numbers added up. Goddesses, Inc. had 216 points. The Avada Kedavras were at 218. And Beast Squad had 511-and-a-half.

CLAUDIA

So Beast Squad had a 500-point Deondra photo and...basically nothing else?

AKASH

Pretty much. They had a Deondra photo, a taxicab receipt, and half credit for the Wall Street bull and Statue of Liberty pics. Because there was only half a Calvin in them.

CLAUDIA

And Goddesses, Inc. didn't have a Deondra photo after all?

AKASH

No, they had a photo. But it got disqualified. Because the list specifically said "photo of Calvin the Cat getting KISSED by Deondra."

And the photo they had was of Deondra HUGGING Calvin the Cat.

PHOTO OF DEONDRA HUGGING CALVIN
(should be here, but Athena wouldn't let me
use it unless I paid her $500)

ATHENA COHEN, Fembot/Goddesses, Inc.
team member (had to pay her $20 for this interview)

Okay, I'm, like, it's just, like...I'm sorry, but I am STILL speechless. Because it was SO INCREDIBLY RIDICULOUS.

Like, have you ever even MET a person as famous and important as Deondra?

I am sure you haven't. But I have met a LOT of them. Okay? And this is the thing about famous people: you don't get to tell them what to do.

Okay?

So if you're like, "Excuse me, Miss Deondra, but I'm a huge fan, and could you please just stop eating your kale salad and kiss this stuffed animal while I take a photo?"

And she's, like, "Okay, whatevs." Which, by the way—MAJOR accomplishment to even get that far. Like, nobody else in that stupid hunt even got in the same ROOM as Deondra. Okay?

But so, like, if Deondra takes your Calvin, and then she HUGS it—and you're about to be all, "Could you actually kiss it instead?" But then her bodyguard or whoever's, like, "JUST TAKE THE PICTURE, KID!"

And then Deondra, like, hands the Calvin back to you and goes, "Have a great day!" and picks up her fork, like, "OVER"—

I'm sorry, but when that happens, you can't be all, "Yeah, um, Deondra? Could you please just, like, do it all over again, only with kissing?"

IT DOESN'T WORK THAT WAY WITH FAMOUS PEOPLE.

Not like you'd know.

CLAUDIA

Wow, Athena. I am SO sorry it went down like that.   ↑
                    (sarcasm)

ATHENA

Whatever, Claudia. You have no idea. Go ride your little pink scooter off a cliff.

CLAUDIA

So after Akash told Mrs. Cohen why the Deondra photo got disqualified, she started yelling, "That's absurd! What's the difference between hugging and kissing?"

AKASH

And Mrs. Bevan—who was using her

official speak-softly-to-the-crazy-parent voice—said, "I believe there's a material distinction."

And Mrs. Cohen was like, "A MATERIAL distinction?"

Then James Mantolini—who, by the way, is clinically insane for going head-to-head with Mrs. Cohen, because that woman is FIERCE—goes, "There's DEFINITELY a difference between hugging and kissing. Let me give you a 'for instance.'..."

JAMES

All I did was point out that Xander had just hugged me in front of the whole school. And I was totally cool with that—

XANDER

It was a Bro-hug. J-MO'S MY BOY!

JAMES

But if he'd KISSED me in front of everybody...that would have been awkward. Especially if it was on the lips.

XANDER

True dat!

AKASH

    Mrs. Cohen was like, "Spare me the lecture, kid!"

    Then she turned on James and was like, "I suppose YOUR Deondra photo has kissing?"

JAMES

    I said, "As a matter of fact, it does."

    And she said, "Well, I would very much like to see that."

    Although her tone of voice kind of made it sound like, "I would very much like to slit you open and pull out your entrails." entrails = guts

    And I was like, "Don't mind if I do."

So I showed her my Deondra photo.

JAMES'S 500-POINT DEONDRA PHOTO

(James's kindergarten Calvin that he got from home)

(woman named Deondra)

AKASH

And THAT brought the ruckus.

CLAUDIA

Athena's mom took one look at the photo and screamed, "THAT'S NOT DEONDRA!" so loud it actually hurt my ears.

And she had a point. Because it was definitely NOT a photo of global pop superstar Deondra Williams.

JAMES

No argument there. And I was expecting some controversy about that. Which is why I took the second photo.

That's Deondra Anthony. She works with my dad. And she's pretty cool. I owe her a huge favor. Or at least my dad does. Which is why she made me take the third picture.

YOU OWE ME FOR This One, GARY!

(Gary = James's dad = Gary Mantolini)

CLAUDIA

Seeing Deondra Anthony's desk plate did NOT make Mrs. Cohen any less angry.

In fact, it made her more angry.

She started yelling, "THAT DOESN'T COUNT! It's got to be THE Deondra! You can't get 500 points for some random Deondra off the street!"

AKASH

Mrs. Bevan—who I'm pretty sure was

enjoying this—waited until Athena's mom
stopped to take a breath.

And then she was like, "If I could just
interject...the list didn't actually specify
that it be THE Deondra. It simply said 'Deondra.'
So technically, it could be ANY Deondra."

CLAUDIA

That basically sent Mrs. Cohen into
sputtering-rage territory. She started yelling
things like, "OH, THAT IS ABSURD!" and "YOU
CAN'T BE SERIOUS!"

And my personal favorite, "THE 'THE'
IS IMPLIED!"

Then James said what everybody was
thinking, but nobody else had the guts to say
to Mrs. Cohen's face.

JAMES

I said, "Hey, lady—I'm not a Harvard-
trained lawyer like you are? But I can read
English. And you're pretty much out of luck
here."

AKASH

That was a beautiful and terrifying thing.
James Mantolini FOR THE WIN.

After that, it was all over but the shouting. And the lawsuit threats. Which Athena's mom clearly did not follow through on, because otherwise I would've been subpoenaed by now.

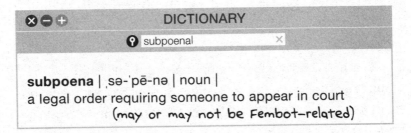

subpoena | ˌsə-ˈpē-nə | noun |
a legal order requiring someone to appear in court
(may or may not be Fembot-related)

CLAUDIA

I think it helped that the Fembots weren't even in second place—so if Mrs. Cohen had managed to get James's photo disqualified, it just would've meant Kalisha's team won.

REESE

I wasn't really following that whole fight. It was pretty confusing. All I knew was, by the time the dust settled, I still had a front-row ticket to MSG in my pants.

WHICH WAS AWESOME!!!!

CLAUDIA

If you ask me, the real victims in this were Kalisha and the Avada Kedavras—who'd beaten a team that had four chauffeured cars and unlimited money. That's pretty superhuman.

KALISHA

It all came down to the Cronut. I guess Goddesses, Inc. figured if they waved enough money around, the bakery would sell them one. But the thing with Cronuts is, they only bake them once a day. Once they're gone, they're gone. After that, all the money in the world won't buy you a Cronut.

CLAUDIA

How did you guys get one?

KALISHA

We pre-ordered ours a week in advance.

CLAUDIA

SERIOUSLY?! How'd you know it'd be on the list?

KALISHA

Basic psychology. We knew Akash was making up the list, so we tried to get inside his head and predict what he'd put on it.

Which is actually not hard with Akash, because he's super-opinionated and really loud.

AKASH

This is true. My Cronut obsession is a matter of public record.

KALISHA

Cronuts weren't the only thing. We reserved a bunch of stuff we didn't end up using. Statue of Liberty tickets, brunch at the American Girl store, that special exhibition at MoMA...

CLAUDIA

But how'd you beat a team that was driving FOUR cars?

KALISHA

Logistics. We divided the list geographically by subway lines. That's the great thing about New York City—you don't HAVE to drive. The subway's awesome.

CLAUDIA

Wow. I am seriously impressed.

Although I have to say—I'm kind of surprised you didn't think of the whole take-a-picture-of-a-non-famous-Deondra thing. I mean, considering how smart you are—

KALISHA

Oh, I definitely THOUGHT of it. I just didn't know anybody named Deondra. Do you?

CLAUDIA

Actually...yeah. There's a Deondra who lives in my building.

I just, um...didn't think of it.

KALISHA

Oh. Wow. Too bad I wasn't on your team. The two of us together could've, y'know...

CLAUDIA

Yeah.

KALISHA

No hard feelings, though. I really enjoyed the mocha latte I got with our Starbucks gift card.

And tell your brother congratulations
again for winning.

CLAUDIA
Yeah.

REESE
WHOOOOOOOOOOOOOOOOOOOOOOOOOOOOO!

CLAUDIA
Cut it out, Reese. Seriously.

EPILOGUE
A WHOLE BUNCH OF
VALUABLE LESSONS

CLAUDIA

In addition to being a hugely
successful fundraiser for a very good cause,
the scavenger hunt was an important learning
experience. And not just for me.

For example, I think all of us learned
you can't trust the media not to completely
exaggerate everything. So if something crazy
goes down and you had anything at all to do
with it, DON'T TALK TO REPORTERS.

**DIMITRI SHARANSKY, The Knights Who Say Ni
team member**

I got my name in the paper!

**TOBY ZIMMERMAN, The Knights Who Say Ni
team member**

Me too! That was beast.

CLAUDIA

Uh, guys? Do you realize that article
single-handedly destroyed the scavenger

hunt? So your talking to that reporter
basically cost the Manhattan Food Bank
millions of dollars in future donations?

DIMITRI

　　Aw, geez...I didn't think of that.

CLAUDIA

　　Also, nobody under sixty-five reads a
newspaper anymore.

TOBY

　　Harsh! Way to make us feel bad, Claudia.

CLAUDIA

　　I just want to make sure we all learn
from our mistakes, Toby.

　　On a personal level, I learned that
when you're putting together a team, it is
very important to choose the ABSOLUTELY BEST
person for the job.

　　And the best person MIGHT be someone
you are going out with.

　　But not necessarily.

JENS

　　I learned that kids from New York

will sometimes make a fun game very, very serious. And sometimes, they even make it too serious.

Also, if you go for a scavenger hunt, it is better not to wear good shoes.

CARMEN

I learned that if your friend tries to jam you with a terrible idea, you should stand your ground and absolutely refuse to let her boyfriend be on your scavenger hunt team.

NOT my boyfriend!
(FOR MILLIONTH TIME)

PARVATI

Ohmygosh, that is EXACTLY the same lesson I learned!

Plus I learned that Kalisha Hendricks is DEFS the smartest person in our class.

CARMEN

What a coincidence! I learned that, too!

CLAUDIA

Okay, whatever. Moving on.

JAMES

I learned to always read the fine print.

Also, don't jump in the back of an open truck.

CLAUDIA

Speaking of fine print, I also learned—although I think it's actually more important that certain OTHER people learn this particular lesson—that there's a time and a place for humor. But it's not always appropriate in every situation.

For example, "the middle of a list of scavenger hunt items" is NOT a good place for humor.

AKASH

I learned that people are idiots who can't take a joke.

What?

Don't look at me like that, Claudia. I regret nothing.

DAD

I learned the importance of being completely honest at all times. Especially when you're texting your wife.

Dad also "doing some soul-searching re: work-life balance" (i.e., wants to quit his job)

REESE

I'll tell you what I learned: no matter how far down you are, you should never, ever quit.

Because you can make it happen! YOU CAN BE THE MIRACLE!

You just gotta believe in yourself.

CLAUDIA

You do realize you had absolutely nothing to do with winning those tickets, right, Reese?

REESE

Ouch! Looks like I also learned some people are sore losers.

CLAUDIA

Reese: not counting the Deondra photo, you got eleven and a half points. Out of a possible two hundred and fifty.

You had a thirty-point item in your hands...AND YOU ATE IT.

REESE

Haters gonna hate, Claude.

But you know what? Totally serious? No kidding around?

It was a great thing you did, creating that scavenger hunt. You worked really, really hard on it.

And yeah, it got a little crazy. But you raised a whole bunch of money for a really important cause. And I KNOW that money made people's lives better.

So you should really be proud of yourself. I'm for sure proud of you.

CLAUDIA

Wow...Thanks, Reese.

REESE

You're totally welcome.

And you know what? Even though all you ever did was badmouth my team and talk about how we were so pathetic, there was no way we'd ever win...for all that hard work you did, you deserve my front-row ticket. I want you to have it.

CLAUDIA

Seriously?

REESE

No.

Ohmygosh, the look on your face when you thought I was going to give it to you? Hilarious!

CLAUDIA

I am turning off the voice memo app now.
Then I'm going to count to five.
And then I'm coming to kill you.

REESE

BYE!
(ran away)

(locked himself in bedroom)

(begged Mom to come save him)

(will pay for this someday)

SPECIAL THANKS

Trevor Williams, Yvette Durant, Alec Lipkind,
Fernando Estevez, Rahm Rodkey, Dafna Sarnoff,
Tal Rodkey, Ronin Rodkey, Jesse Barrett, Anna
Rose Meisenzahl, Kai Nieuwenhof, Mustafa the
Tailor, Liz Casal, Lisa Clark, Chris Goodhue,
Russ Busse, Andrea Spooner, Josh Getzler,
and The Greatest City On Earth.

RIP

The FAO Schwarz store at 767 5th Avenue (1986-2015).
Will probably be replaced by a Duane Reade.
(See page 132.)

PHOTO CREDITS

All photographs are copyright © 2015 by Geoff Rodkey
except for the following, reprinted with permission.

p. 20: Currier & Ives N.Y.
p. 28: pop_jop/iStock
pp. 141, 142, 146, 147, 148, 149: Jesse Garrett
p. 189: dageldob/iStock
p. 215: Underlying image: wavebreak/iStock

ILLUSTRATION CREDITS

Liz Casal: pp. iii, 1, 2, 6, 8, 13, 22, 26, 33, 35,
37, 46, 53, 60, 61, 68, 76, 88, 100, 108, 110, 114,
126, 138, 151, 154, 165, 169, 174, 177, 187, 196,
197, 202, 206, 212, 223, 233, 239, 250, 255, 261
Lisa Clark: pp. 11, 15
Chris Goodhue, maps: pp. 6, 31, 69, 77, 95, 101, 127,
138, 157, 166, 176

COMING IN FALL 2016!
JUST IN TIME FOR THE ACTUAL
US PRESIDENTIAL ELECTION!

THE TAPPER TWINS RUN FOR PRESIDENT

(Of the sixth grade.
Not the whole country.
But still—it gets pretty crazy.)

Turn the page—or swipe left on your
electronic book-type thing—
to read the beginning!

PROLOGUE

CLAUDIA

My name is Claudia Tapper. I'm twelve years old. And I'm just going to be completely honest about this: I want to be president.

And not just president of the sixth grade, but the whole United States.

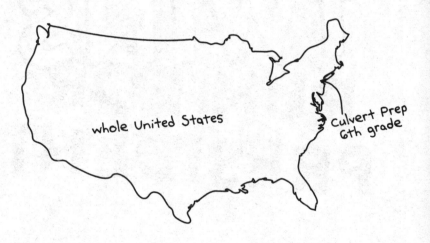

whole United States

Culvert Prep 6th grade

I know this probably sounds obnoxious. But I think it's very important to set big goals ← for yourself and try to be the best person you can be. That way, even if you fall short, you could still end up being vice president.

(I also want to be a famous singer-songwriter—but that is a whole other story)

∟ or maybe governor of something

I also know getting elected president is a MAJOR long shot, and I'll have to face a ton of challenges to pull it off. For the record, I am totally fine with that. Facing big challenges and kicking butt at them is what makes a person a strong leader. Nobody wants a president who didn't have to work hard to get the job.

President Warren G. Harding (1921–23):
didn't have to work v. hard to get job—
WAS TERRIBLE AT IT (srsly—google him)

That's why I decided to put together this book, which is the official history of my campaign to be re-elected president of Culvert Prep's sixth grade class.

Because that election was the biggest challenge of my life.

Mostly thanks to my stupid twin brother.

REESE

I seriously was NOT planning to run for president.

I mean, it's not like I want to be one when I grow up. I've seen the real president on TV, and there's no way I'd want that guy's job. He spends his whole day wearing a suit and getting yelled at. It's even worse than being a lawyer. *not true. Dad is a lawyer— it is MUCH worse than being presider*

But the thing is, sometimes you have to stand up for your beliefs. And that's what I was doing.

This election wasn't about me.

It was about freedom. *Reese HAS NO CLUE what that even means (his campaign manager taught him to say it)*

MOM AND DAD (Text messages copied from Dad's phone)

← MOM

FYI, Claudia's writing another oral history ← — oral history=my interviews w/everybody involved

DAD → My whole body just clenched up in fear

I told her she can't use our texts this time

Smart move. We would look like worst parents ever

No kidding. Especially me

Just don't leave your phone lying around or she will steal it and take screenshots

Don't worry—my phone is password-protected

↑ Dad's password=7734

CHAPTER 1:
DOGGIE TERROR
FROM THE SKIES

CLAUDIA

None of this ever would have happened if Reese hadn't almost murdered a very small dog with a soccer ball.

REESE

I did NOT almost murder it! The dog didn't even get hurt!

And it was a total accident! So even if I'd skronked the dog, it wouldn't have been murder. It would've been, like... ~~not a real word~~

dogslaughter.

←——(like "manslaughter," but with dog?)
(either way, not a real word)

CLAUDIA

I should back up a little and explain the situation.

Reese and I live in New York City. Which is awesome. It's actually TOO awesome, because so many people want to live here that it is seriously overcrowded.

And it's not just overcrowded in the
subway, or the grocery store, or Midtown
during the holidays, but everywhere. There
is just no space at all.

Midtown during holidays=INSANELY CROWDED

For example: size-wise, my bedroom is
somewhere between a very tiny closet and a
very large shoebox.

Not that I'm complaining. I'm actually
very grateful I even HAVE a bedroom. If
Reese and I had to share a room, it would
be a total nightmare. For a LOT of reasons.
But especially because he smells horrible.

REESE

Okay, THAT is not fair. I only smell
bad after soccer.

CLAUDIA

Reese, you play soccer EVERY SINGLE DAY.

REESE

No way! I play, like, five days a week.
Tops.

CLAUDIA

Okay, so—FIVE out of seven days, you
smell like a butt...that's been stuffed inside
a moldy shoe...with some rotten vegetables.

REESE

Yeah. But only five.

CLAUDIA

I am getting seriously off track here.
My point is, New York City is SO overcrowded
that sometimes normal things end up in not-
normal places. Like our school's playground.
Which, instead of being in a normal place—
like next to the parking lot—is on the roof.
Five stories up.

(also, there's no parking lot)

And if you are insane enough to get into a contest to see who can kick a soccer ball over the rooftop fence—

rooftop fence
(actually more of a wall)
(looks kind of like a prison)
(probably on purpose)

REESE

It wasn't a contest! It was a bet. And the bet was I couldn't do a bicycle kick from in front of the SOUTH fence that was high enough to clear the whole NORTH fence— which was ridic hard, 'cause it was January and I was wearing snow boots. So it's totally beast that I nailed it.

Now that I think of it, Xander still owes me five bucks for that.

CLAUDIA

Like I was saying: if you're insane
enough to kick your soccer ball over the
rooftop fence, New York City's SO overcrowded
that even if you DON'T actually take out some
mean rich lady's equally mean little dog
while she's walking it down 77th Street...

MEAN RICH LADY/
MEAN LITTLE DOG

the ball will come screaming down out of
the sky and scare BOTH the mean little dog
AND the mean rich lady SO MUCH that
she'll march into Culvert Prep and
demand to talk to whoever's in charge of
not letting soccer balls fly off the roof.

dog was
very mean
EVEN BEFORE
this happened
(so was
owner)

And THAT is how Vice Principal Bevan wound up banning soccer from the roof.

REESE

Which was totally cray! That was, like, a straight-up attack on my _freedom._ And my _liberty_. And my _human rights_ to, like, kick soccer balls during free time.

And that's why I got into _politics._

srsly, Reese has NO CLUE what all these words even mean

CHAPTER 2:
OUR APARTMENT HAS A
SUPREME LEADER ^

(And Other Stuff You Should Know About Politics)

CLAUDIA

In case you're like my brother and have no idea what politics even is, it's all about who gets to decide the really important questions in a country and/or middle school. Like "Should soccer balls be banned from the roof?" Or "What if we invade Canada?"

There are a bunch of ways politics can work. But the two most common ones are "dictatorship" and "democracy."

In a dictatorship, one person ← (i.e., the dictator) decides everything. Then everybody else has to do whatever that person says. It's VERY unfair.

Two good examples of dictatorships are North Korea and our apartment.

REESE

The dictator of our apartment is Mom. But she's pretty cool about it.

↑
Dad not happy about this

CLAUDIA

It is definitely much better to live in our apartment than North Korea. For one thing, we have totally uncensored Internet access. Mostly because Mom couldn't figure out the parental control app. ↙ (Dad's hours are even crazier/longer)

Plus, she works crazy-long hours. So most of the time, Ashley, our after-school sitter, is the substitute dictator. And tbh, Ashley is a total pushover. For example, last year she let Reese eat nothing but Cheezy Puffs for dinner for three straight weeks.

I am still a little surprised that didn't kill him.

cheezy Puffs (will srsly kill you if you eat enough)

REESE

It ALMOST did. By the end, I think my skin was turning orange.

CLAUDIA

The second kind of politics is a democracy, where everybody gets to vote on all the important questions. ← (U.S.A. population)

But in a country of 320,000,000 people— or even a sixth grade of 97 people—letting everybody vote on everything is way too complicated. So instead, everybody votes on who their leaders should be, and then the leaders make the decisions.

← (FYI: this is called "representative" democracy)

REESE

So is school a dictatorship? Or a democracy? 'Cause we defs don't have uncensored Internet access. You can't get on ANY good sites from the cafeteria Wi-Fi.

CLAUDIA

Culvert Prep is a mix. It's basically 90% dictatorship and 10% democracy.

Culvert Prep
(90% dictatorship)

(rooftop playground/prison
is over here)

REESE

Who's the dictator of Culvert Prep?
Vice Principal Bevan?

CLAUDIA

No, it's the Head of School, Ms.
Tingley. Plus Principal Spooner. Vice
Principal Bevan's more like their army.
Like, whenever there's rioting in the
streets, they send her in to restore order.

REESE

I have no clue what you're talking
about. All I know is, Mrs. Bevan's the one
who banned soccer balls from the roof.
And when me and Xander and Wyatt were like,

"Puhhhleeeeaase let us play soccer on the roof again!" she was all, "Why don't you ask your class rep to bring it up in SG?"

SG = Student Government

CLAUDIA

Student Government is the 10% democracy part of Culvert Prep Middle School. SG is made up of one representative (a "rep") from each homeroom class, plus a president and a treasurer for each grade.

The class rep for Reese's homeroom is my second-best friend Carmen.

tied with Parvati.
So, rank is:
1. Sophie
2. Carmen (tie)
2. Parvati (tie)

CARMEN GUTIERREZ, 6th grade class rep/second-best friend of Claudia

So your brother and his friends come up to me at lunch, and they're like, "You GOTTA get the SG to tell Mrs. Bevan to let us play soccer on the roof!"

But the thing is, I've been trying to get Culvert Prep to install solar panels on the roof FOR-EVER. Solar power's MAJOR for our future—if we don't stop burning coal and oil, the ice caps are going to melt, New York City's going to be totally underwater, and we're ALL GOING TO DROWN.

CLAUDIA

Carmen is VERY concerned about global warming. It's basically the whole reason she ran for class rep.

CARMEN

It's been ridic hard to get solar panels approved. Whenever I'd bring it up in SG, Mr. McDonald would be like, "There's just so much sports playing on the roof that I don't know if it's really practical."

Mr. McDonald = SG's faculty advisor

So I saw this soccer ban as a MAJOR opportunity. And I was like, "I'm sorry, Reese. The future of human civilization's at stake here."

And Reese was like, "So's our soccer game!"

So I said, "Maybe you should discuss it with someone else in SG."

And he was like, "Who?"

And I was like, "Duh! The class president."

CLAUDIA

And at that moment, the class president was me.

Read the rest of the story in
THE TAPPER TWINS RUN FOR PRESIDENT
Coming September 2016!

ABOUT THE AUTHOR

Geoff Rodkey is best known as the
screenwriter of the hit films *Daddy Day
Care*, *RV*, and the Disney Channel's *Good
Luck Charlie, It's Christmas*. The author of
the acclaimed middle-grade adventure-comedy
trilogy *The Chronicles of Egg*, he's also
written for the educational video game *Where
in the World Is Carmen Sandiego?*, the non-
educational MTV series *Beavis and Butt-Head*,
Comedy Central's *Politically Incorrect*, and
at least two magazines that no longer exist.

    Geoff currently lives in New York City
with his wife and three sons, none of whom
bear any resemblance whatsoever to the
characters in *The Tapper Twins Tear Up
New York*.